OTHER BOOKS BY KATE L. MARY

The Broken World Series:
Broken World
Shattered World
Mad World
Lost World
New World
Forgotten World
Silent World
Broken Stories

The Twisted Series:
Twisted World
Twisted Mind
Twisted Memories
Twisted Fate

The Outliers Saga:
Outliers
Uprising

The Blood Will Dry

Collision

When We Were Human

Alone: A Zombie Novel

SILENT WORLD

Book Seven in the *Broken World* Series

KATE L. MARY

Twisted Press

Published by Twisted Press, LLC, an independently owned company.

Copyright © 2016 by Kate L. Mary
ISBN-13: 978-1533654687
ISBN-10: 1533654689
Edited by Emily Teng
Cover art by Kate L. Mary

CHAPTER ONE

JIM

Every breath I let out echoes through my head, and the harder my heart pounds, the louder it seems to thump against my eardrums. The constant pounding isn't a bad thing, though. Anything that can drown out the noise of the zombies barreling down on me is more than welcome.

Just keep going. Just keep running.

I've never really been one for pep talks, but it's all I can think as I charge through the field, leaving the farmhouse behind for good. Saying goodbye to the promise of safety in Atlanta and the friends I've made who are quite possibly the only good people left in this whole Godforsaken world. It's for a good cause. I know it is. Doesn't mean I don't hate that I'm rushing into the dark unknown with little chance of making it out of this alive. Because, let's face it, carpet and duct tape will only keep you safe for so long when you're facing a world overtaken by zoms.

When a pang shoots through my side, the grunt I let out would rival even the moans of the dead. I press my leather-gloved hands against the rug wrapped around my stomach, trying to hold myself together while I focus on keeping my legs pumping. Left, right, left, right, left, right. It's all I can concentrate on right now. Moving forward, one foot after the other. Ignoring the pain in my legs, the pressure in my lungs, and the pounding of the feet at my back.

The moon above me is bright enough that it should light the way, but it doesn't help all that much. Axl and Angus did a good job of wrapping me up, which means I should be safe from the jaws of the dead, but it also means it's tough to see anything that isn't right in front of me. The layers of scarves and duct tape have made peripheral vision a thing of the past, and I'm looking at the world with what feels like tunnel vision as I rush toward the trees in front of me. Doesn't matter. All I have to do is outrun the dead and find a safe place to hide.

Yeah, that's *all* I have to do.

I keep moving. Through the field and into the forest, jumping over fallen branches and anything else that might trip me up. The toe of my right foot hits some debris buried by long-dead leaves and I stumble a few steps, but I force my body to stay upright. Keep my legs moving and my feet firmly planted on the ground. If I fall, the carpet and tape should keep me from being ripped apart, but there's no guarantee the zombies will get tired of me any time soon. Getting back up will be impossible once I'm surrounded by the horde.

After what feels like an hour of running, I finally break through the trees. Light glimmers off the water in front of me, and I skitter to a stop. My hand is still pressed to my side—barely holding me together—and my lungs threaten to burst with every breath I take, but all I can do is focus on the water in front of me as I try to figure out what to do next.

The river doesn't look that deep, and it can't be more than twenty feet to the other side. I could make it. It could give me the advantage I've been looking for. Of course, if I fall, there's also a good chance the current will sweep me farther downstream or pull me under. With the layers and layers of fabric taped to my body, I could very easily drown in just a foot of water. Maybe even less.

Leaves rustle behind me, and I turn long enough to see the branches at my back move. That's all it takes to make up my mind. The river is a risk, but I'd rather face the current than the zombies heading my way.

I move, charging into the water without giving it a second thought. Liquid that's barely above freezing seeps inside the strips of carpet taped to my legs and fills my shoes. Within seconds my skin is covered in goose bumps. It's an odd mixture. My body sweating under the layers of fabric while shivering at the same time. Like I've been sucked into some kind of alternate universe.

Shit, that's a dumb thought. Aren't the zombies trying to rip me to pieces enough to make me think I've been sucked into some kind of twisted world where nothing makes sense?

The current is stronger than I anticipated or my legs are weaker. Either way, less than three steps into the water and I'm already wobbling. I hold my arms up like I'm walking on a balance beam, and each time I lift a foot I'm careful to make my steps short and close together. It makes the going slow, but it also keeps me from tumbling into the water and being swept away.

By the time the first zombie splashes into the river at my back, the water is up to my knees. Without thinking, I turn. So fast that it causes me to lose my balance. Panic that's stronger than the current under me clenches my gut as I tumble forward, throwing my hands out. The freezing water engulfs me and my head goes under, but I keep my arms and legs rigid. Even as my mouth and nose are filled with icy liquid, I force my body to stay firm, refusing to allow myself to panic and lose control of the situation.

When I lift my head from the freezing water, I'm face to face with so many zombies that it would be impossible to count them all. Like me, the river seems to have frozen most of them in place. The few that have ventured in wobble with each step, and even though I know I should get up and move, I stay on all fours where I am and watch. My breath held as I wait. Praying for the outcome that will mean I made the right decision.

The zombie closest to me stumbles and then falls, dipping under for a few seconds before resurfacing further downstream. His arms flail as he's carried off, and the moan he lets out sounds so oddly human that it makes the hair on my head prickle. I'm still watching him float away when a second, and then a third, bite the dust.

Watching those bastards get swept away is all it takes to snap me out of it.

I have to get up. Have to get on my feet and keep moving. Once I'm on the other side, I should be home free.

Staying on all fours, I turn until my back is once again to the advancing dead. Then I move forward, keeping my head up and my eyes on the shore in front of me. I'm halfway across when the water gets too deep and I'm forced to push myself up. It takes a lot of effort, and when I make it back to my feet, it feels like I weigh a hundred pounds more than I did before I stepped into the river. Every step takes an insane amount of effort, but every inch is a victory I've won over the zombies.

You can make it. You're almost there.

By the time I'm able to reach out and touch the shore, my legs are almost numb, but it isn't until I'm lying on my back in the grass and overcome with tremors that I realize why. I'm freezing, and my teeth are chattering so hard that I wouldn't be surprised if they shattered.

I stay where I am, shivering and gasping, staring up at the dark sky. It's so clear that every star is visible, and the moon is so big and bright that it seems like I could almost reach out and touch it. The world around me is silent other than my pounding heart and the rush of the river at my feet.

When the thumping in my ears has subsided, I finally remember the zombies. I push myself up and blink, but even then it takes me a few seconds to register what I'm seeing. The bank on the other side of the water is empty, and so is the river in front of me. Where they all went, I don't have a damn clue, but I know I got lucky. There wasn't a part of me that thought I would make it out of this alive when I volunteered to lead that horde away, but it seems like someone is looking out for me.

Not that I'm out of the woods yet. With the way the water has soaked into this carpet, not to mention how cold it is, I'm liable to die of pneumonia if I don't get dry fast.

I pull out my knife and get to work on the tape that's wrapped around my head. There's a shit ton of it though, and the more I cut the more I risk slicing off a piece of my skull. I let out a deep breath, hoping to calm my pounding heart as I take a few seconds to study my surroundings. Other than the river and the chattering of my teeth, everything is as silent as a graveyard. So quiet, in fact, that it's kind of creepy. Like I'm the only living person in the whole damn world.

The extra padding covering my ears isn't going to help me hear if something does decide to sneak up on me. I have to get this shit off my head and then work on the rest of me. Getting warm and dry is one of the most important things I can do at the moment.

I go back to trying to cut the duct tape from my head, but it only takes me a few seconds to give up. My gaze moves to my legs, and I shift so I can get a better look at the situation. The carpet wrapped around my lower half should be easier to get off. For one, I can see what I'm doing, but also because there's a gap on the inside of my legs where I should be able to slice the tape off.

Hoping to get a better angle, I spread my legs wider, then slip the blade of my knife under the carpet on my right leg and move it down slowly, cutting the tape wrapped around my upper thigh. It slices through the silver strips, and the carpet comes free. I pull it off and toss it aside before moving to my left thigh. This time, I slide my blade faster through the first strip of tape before moving on to the second one. My blade is four inches above my knee and halfway through the last piece of tape on my thigh when a sharp pain pulses through my leg.

"Shit."

I suck in a deep breath and take a quick look around before moving my knife down the rest of the way. Once the tape has been cut, I toss the carpet aside and twist my leg so I can get a good look at my inner thigh. A dark red spot has spread across my jeans, growing bigger by the second, and there's a slice in the fabric about three inches long. I stick my fingers in the hole and pull, ripping the jeans a little more so I can get a better look. Blood seeps from the cut, but without a flashlight it's impossible to know how bad it is. Bad enough that if these were different times, I'd be on my way to the emergency room. But bad enough to kill me? It's hard to tell.

Either way, I'm going to have to do something to stop the bleeding.

The scarf wrapped around my head seems like the perfect solution, so I go back to pulling at it for a few seconds before giving up. The leather gloves taped to my hands are too bulky, making it almost impossible to feel what I'm doing.

Have to get the gloves off first.

Whoever taped the gloves on my hands did a helluva job, and it takes me a good ten minutes to get the right one off. Once that's done, though, I'm able to get a better sense of where the tape ends and the gloves begin, which means I get the second glove cut off in half the time. Every move I make causes the cut on my leg to throb, and even without a flashlight, I can tell it's bleeding like crazy by how much bigger the spot on my jeans has gotten.

I go back to working on my head, and now that my hands are free, cutting off the scarves and hat isn't nearly as hard. Once the scarves are off I untangle them, pulling free every little bit of tape that's stuck to the fabric. Then I wrap one of the scarves around my thigh three times before tying it off, wincing when the scratchy material rubs against the open wound on my leg. It hurts like hell, but there's not a whole lot I can do about it out in the open like this. I need to get up, get moving, and find a place to hold up for the night so I can get some rest.

I start to climb to my feet, but moving isn't easy with the carpet still strapped to my torso, arms, and lower legs. Getting it off is going to take me a good bit of time—longer than I should risk being this exposed—so instead of staying where I am and working to get free, I haul myself up and start moving. The rest of this shit can wait until I find somewhere to hide out for the night.

"There has to be a house or two around here somewhere. Right? This is America." Or was, anyway.

I don't know how long I ran—a couple miles at least—but I do know the farmhouse I left behind is no longer occupied by anything but ghosts. The others were probably gone within seconds of me running out the door. That was the deal, anyway. I lead the dead away and they haul ass to Atlanta. Save the world.

Shit. I hope it works.

Thinking about them is what keeps me moving. Even when my limbs start to tremble so much that it's difficult to stay upright. Vivian, Axl, Angus, Joshua, and Parvarti. Then there's Megan. She's the real reason I offered to lead the zombies away. Not only did I make a promise to her dad, but seeing that little baby was a reminder of exactly what we're fighting for. Hope and a future that isn't full of death.

Every step I take seems to make my limbs heavier. Almost as if I'm dragging the weight of the world with me. I keep at it, though, and before long the horizon has gotten orange. A little more walking and the color has spread, moving across the sky and bleeding into the darkness above me. Drowning out the stars until they're invisible.

I'm gasping and shivering by the time the sun is all the way over the horizon, and it isn't until then that I spot a cluster of houses in the distance. I don't know where I am or how long it's going to take me to get to Atlanta from here, but I do know my best bet is to get to a town and find a map. Hopefully, those houses mean there's a gas station or convenience store nearby.

I force my legs to move faster, dragging myself forward until the houses come into view. There are a couple dozen homes, all pretty close together, but that's about it. No signs that indicate there are any businesses. Great.

I pause and let out a deep breath. It's early, and even though I've been up all night, the idea of stopping now doesn't feel right. I should take advantage of the daylight and move a little further. We were headed east, and with the sun up, I know which direction it is. It makes sense to keep going.

"You can do this."

Talking to myself makes me feel dumb as shit, but it also makes me feel better for some reason. The utter silence surrounding me is unsettling. The world should have noise. Cars, planes, or kids. Hell, I'd settle for people screaming at each other. Lord knows it wouldn't be anything unusual for me. Between the way I grew up and the years spent behind bars, I'm used to hearing people fight. But this? The total silence that has fallen over the world scares the shit out of me.

I pass the grouping of houses and head toward the sun. Dragging my throbbing, heavy limbs across the open field to the road. When my feet hit the blacktop, I feel a little better. A little more normal. Despite the wet carpet clinging to my body and the sweat dripping down my back, there's something ordinary about the open road. Like I'm just a traveler out looking for a new life instead of a guy running from the dead. Like if I can just walk far enough, I'll reach a destination worth all this trouble.

A guy can dream, anyway.

I keep moving, but the higher the sun gets, the more I start to sweat. Crazy thing is, I haven't warmed up completely. The carpet scraps aren't going to dry out any time soon, and the Georgia sun is hotter than hell against my exposed face. The air I breathe in gets thicker by the minute and beads of sweat drip from my forehead into my eyes every other second, but there are still goose bumps on my arms.

Every step makes my leg throb a little more, but I don't stop to look at the cut until sometime after what should be lunch. My stomach is growling so hard I'm surprised it hasn't drawn every zombie in a ten-mile radius my way, but there's also an uneasiness in it that makes me think I'd most likely throw up any food I did try to eat. Not that I have any.

I lower myself down on the side of the road, laying my knife right next to me just in case, and then gently unwrap the scarf. The dried blood has glued the damn thing to my leg, and not only does it hurt like hell when I pull it away, but the cut starts oozing again. I suck in a deep breath and dab at the fresh blood, getting my first good look at the damage since the sun came up. It's deep and long. Four inches, maybe. What really worries me are the red streaks under my skin, moving from the cut to the other parts of my leg. I know infection when I see one, but it just doesn't make any sense. I cut myself six hours ago, maybe a bit more. It's too soon for infection to have set in. At least I think it is.

"Gotta get someplace safe and get this thing cleaned out."

The sound of my voice in the midst of the quiet makes me jump. I look around, sure something is going to come charging, but the landscape around me is as still and empty as it was when I sat down. If there are zombies nearby, they aren't close enough to hear me talking to myself.

"Doesn't mean they aren't headed this way. I have to keep moving."

I wrap the scarf back around my thigh and tie it off before getting back to my feet. My body seems to sway under the hot sun, and the world around me tilts at an odd angle. I shake my head. I'm tired. That's all it is. I need to rest.

"Next house."

I take off down the road once again, ignoring the way my nose and cheeks burn under the rays of the Georgia sun. The pulse of pain shooting through my leg with every step I take isn't as easy to push aside, though. Every time I lift my left leg, a throb shoots up my thigh, and every time I put my foot on the ground, the same ache moves down to my calf. It's like a seesaw of pain in my leg, and the more I walk the more intense it gets and the more my head starts to pound.

By the time a house comes into view, the sun has moved so it's at my back, which is currently drenched with sweat. Despite that, I've started to shiver so hard that my body is shaking. The place is way off in the distance, and with as heavy as my legs have gotten, I'm not quite sure how I'm going to make it. It's like someone is at my side, adding invisible weights every time I lift my legs. I feel like shit, too, and if I didn't know any better, I'd think I had a fever.

The red lines on my leg come to mind, but I push the thought aside. Infection doesn't happen this fast. It's impossible. It has to be something else.

The world sways, but I force myself to keep moving as I tug at the carpet taped to my body. It's pressing into my lungs like it's trying to crush the life out of me. Or at least that's what it seems like. It's hard to tell, though, with the fogginess in my brain.

I shake my head, trying to clear the cobwebs or dust or whatever it is that's clogging my thoughts. It doesn't help, so I concentrate on the house in front of me. On lifting one leg and putting it in front of the other. Ignoring the throb that has now gotten constant and so intense it's almost blinding. If I can just get inside, I'll be okay. Once I'm in there, I can rest for a few hours. Check out the cut. Maybe even clean it out. Then I'll figure out how to get this carpet off before it crushes me to death.

I just hope to God there aren't any zombies inside. With the way I'm feeling right now, I'm not sure I'd be able to fight even a toddler zom off.

By the time I stumble into the front yard, I'm barely able to stay upright. My temples throb right along with the beat of my heart, and it feels like my head is floating a foot above my shoulders. Every inch of me shakes, while under the layers of clothes and carpet taped to my body, my skin is moist with sweat.

"Shit," I mutter, shoving damp hair out of my face. "I'm sick."

Is the fever raging through my body from the cut, or was it something that has been hiding in my body for the last few days and has just now decided to rear its destructive head? Either way, I know one thing for sure: I'm screwed. It's not like there are doctors or pharmacies anywhere. I'm on my own, and in this world, that can mean the difference between life and death.

When I reach the house, I peer in through the window on the front door. Nothing moves, but it looks like there was a struggle here at some point. Legos are spread across the floor, and a couple chairs are knocked over. From where I'm standing, I can see into the kitchen a bit, and what looks like a bag of flour is lying on its side, its contents spilled across the floor.

Still, as far as I can tell, the place is empty. Not that I have much of a choice about where to go. There are no neighboring houses anywhere in sight, and if I don't get somewhere safe — and soon — I'm liable to fall over. Every second that goes by has me feeling like more cotton has been stuffed into my head, and my legs are already so wobbly that it's hard to walk. I need to find a place to ride this thing out.

11

I turn the doorknob, but it doesn't budge. Not that I'm surprised. Breaking in will be a last resort. The last thing I need is for a zombie to wander inside while I'm delirious with fever. I have to find another way.

I move toward the garage, leaning against the side of the house for support, and turn the corner to find a door right in front of me. Even though I'm sure it's going to be locked, I try the knob. I'm so shocked when it opens that I almost fall right into the dark garage. Somehow, I manage to catch myself before I face plant on the cement floor.

There's an SUV parked in the middle of the two-car garage, but other than a couple bikes and a lawnmower, it's the only vehicle. I leave the door I just came through open and head around the car, but the door that leads into the house is also locked.

I exhale and lean against the wall when the room starts to spin. My head is a mess and my legs are barely keeping me up. The garage won't be comfortable to rest in, and it's so dark I won't be able to check out my injury or see to cut these damn strips of carpet off, but with how I'm feeling, it's going to have to do. At least until I can get some of my energy back.

I go back the way I came, shutting the door and making sure it's locked so nothing can wander in while I'm passed out. Then, without really thinking it through, I pull open the back door to the SUV and climb inside. The leather seats are soft against my cheek when I lay down, and within seconds I can feel myself drifting off.

CHAPTER TWO

AMIRA

The words on the page in front of me start to blur together. I blink, but it doesn't help. Not that it matters. Not only have I read this book a few times already, but I also haven't been able to absorb much—if any—of the last few pages. It's hard focusing on anything but Dad right now.

Five days, that's how long he's been gone. I try to tell myself that he'll be back, but it's hard staying positive when I have no idea what's going on outside the walls of this house. Plus, being all alone like this makes me feel small and young all over again—not twenty-one and nearly a college graduate—and I hate it. Hate how I can't seem to focus on anything but the fact that I'm alone.

When my vision doesn't clear, I close my eyes. They're so tired that they burn, and I know I should rest them, but these books are literally the only things keeping me sane.

Of course, if I read until my eyes fail, I'll be in even deeper shit than I am now.

When I shut the book, my fingers curl around the edges until the cover digs into my skin. The pain barely registers as I stare out the window. Behind the house, the field is so green and fresh with spring that if I didn't know better, I'd think the world was going to start anew.

I do know better, though. Nothing will be new ever again.

When my stomach rumbles, I look away. The early morning sun is so bright that a glowing, yellow ball mars my vision. Even when I close my eyes, it won't go away.

How am I going to make it on my own?

I don't move, don't breath, try not to think, but when no life-altering epiphany comes to mind I finally open my eyes and toss the book aside. No sense focusing on the deep pile of shit I'm living in. Especially not with my stomach begging for food the way it is.

I crawl across the attic on my hands and knees, and dust puffs up around me, tickling my nose. A sneeze threatens to burst out of me, but I sniff it back while pretending that the dirt is also to blame for my watering eyes. The lie is literally impossible to hold on to when I stop in front of the food I have left. Half a protein bar. That's it.

Shit, Dad. What happened to you?

When he left five days ago, he promised he'd be back. He also made me swear that I wouldn't leave the attic until he showed up. Five days later and I'm not just out of food, I'm out of options. I'm going to have to head out to find supplies on my own. The question is: should I go now or wait until it gets dark?

It's impossible to know the right thing to do.

I nibble on the last of my protein bar while I think it through, chewing each bite slowly. Savoring it like it might be the last morsel of food I'll ever have. It's the only way I'll get through this alive, by assuming everything I do or everything I eat will be the last.

The one time Dad let me go out on a run with him, we

went at night. Even though it was tough to see the dead coming, their smell usually gives them away—something I can take advantage of—but a freshly turned zombie nearly bit my head off when he snuck up on me. That was something we hadn't planned on, and it was a close enough call that Dad started leaving me here alone. I wasn't happy about it then, and I'm even less happy about it now that he's missing.

Does that mean I should go during the day?

Probably.

When I've swallowed the last of my protein bar, I strap my knife to my waist and crawl over to the attic door. I count to ten before pushing it open a crack, freezing while my eyes adjust to the bright house below. The plant is still where I left it, lying on its side in the middle of the hall. I study the dark soil that's spread across the carpet, taking my time to look it over. As far as I can tell, everything is exactly the same as last time. No footprints are visible, and it isn't spread any further down the hall than it was when I put it there. Which means the house should be empty. If anyone had come up the stairs, they would have had to walk through the dirt.

I should be good.

Even though I'm fairly certain no one has been inside the house since I crawled into the attic, I stare at the dark soil for a few minutes longer. My heart has started pounding so hard that it thumps against my ribs, and a fine sheen of sweat has broken out across my body. I'm at a distinct disadvantage in this world, and I know it. If I want to survive, I have to take my time. Be cautious and consider every move I make carefully. It's the only way I'll be able to make it to tomorrow.

At least five minutes pass and nothing has changed, so I push the door open a little wider and wait. Still, no one—or nothing—comes running.

I shove the door open the rest of the way and push the ladder down until it extends to the floor. Before I do anything else I count to ten, holding my breath the entire time. Once I'm totally sure nothing is going to jump out and get me, I climb down the ladder.

15

The rickety thing shifts under my weight, giving the impression that it's going to collapse at any second. It won't and I know it, but that doesn't stop me from holding on to the rungs tighter. When I reach the bottom, I pause and inhale slowly, concentrating on the smells. Dirt. Dust. The faint stink of the bathroom at the end of the hall. But no rot. No sign that anything dead has made its way into the house.

I hold on to the ladder while taking a wide step, stretching my right leg over the soil that's spread out on the carpet. When my foot reaches the top step, I lean forward and grab hold of the banister before propelling myself the rest of the way over. Once both of my feet are firmly planted on the stairs, I press my back up against the wall and pull my knife. Freezing in place. Scanning the steps and what little bit of the first floor I can see over the railing. Inhaling. Using every one of the senses I possess to make sure there's nothing dangerous waiting for me.

After a few minutes, I take a hesitant step down. Nothing happens, so I move again. Each step I take is thought out. Calculated. Each breath I inhale comes in through my nose and is analyzed for anything that seems off. Every little bit of the first floor that comes into view is scanned and studied. Searched for anything that doesn't belong. From what I can see, everything is exactly the same as it was the last time I was downstairs. The flour spread across the tile is exactly where I left it and the silverware drawer is still on the floor, its contents spread strategically across the kitchen, and the bucket of Legos is still lying on its side in the living room. The brightly colored blocks are arranged in a pattern that took me a long time to achieve. It's so subtle that no one else would notice it, but spread out in a way that if someone disturbs it, I will know. None of the blocks have moved, though. Good.

When I reach the first floor, I tiptoe my way across the kitchen, careful to avoid the flour and silverware scattered everywhere. In the living room I do the same, making my way through the house to the front window so I can look out across the yard. Clear. No zombies or anything else moving that I can see.

Up until now, we've been lucky. Our house is so far out that we haven't run into much trouble, but I know it won't last forever. Eventually, someone or something will stumble upon this house and decide to search it for supplies. All I can do is hope and pray that whoever finds this place decides to take what they want and move on. But with as secluded as we are, I can't stop from worrying that they'll decide to hang out for a while instead.

It's now or never. I turn away from the window, once again picking my way through the house. I'd rather it be never, but if I want to survive, that can't be the case. It's just me now, which means it's my responsibility to find food, water, and any other supplies I might need.

My backpack is hanging on a hook beside the door leading into the garage, and on the wall above it my name is spelled out in pink letters, left over from my school days. The sight of the empty hook next to it sends a pang shooting through me, and I do everything I can to avoid looking at the name above that now-useless hook. Focusing on my shoes as I pull my bag down, then turning my back to the wall as I unzip it.

I know exactly what's inside my book bag, but I double check my supplies before heading out anyway. Flashlight, small first aid kit, a bottle of water, a pocketknife, house keys, and a box of bullets. The necessities.

Once I'm sure everything is still here, I open the closet and pull Dad's golf bag out from behind the coats. I move the clubs aside until the barrel of the .22 is visible. Just seeing it causes a pang to vibrate through my chest, but I ignore the ache and slide the rifle out so I can sling it over my shoulder. The rifle is a last resort, but having it will make me feel better.

When I turn to face the garage door, I take one last breath, blowing it out slowly. Just like I did when I left the attic, I ease the door open. Breathing in through my nose. Analyzing. Waiting. Searching the dark corners of the room for movement. There isn't any, and I open the door all the way to find everything exactly as I left it. Mom's SUV is parked in the middle of the garage, and everything else perfectly pristine. Undisturbed.

Good.

No time to celebrate, though. I have to move.

The garage is blacker than the pits of hell when I step inside, but I don't need the light to know where I'm going. My bike is to the right of the door, leaning against the wall, and it only takes me a moment to flip the kickstand up and pull it across the room. My heart is beating like mad by the time I have the door open, and it gets even worse when the sunlight nearly blinds me. I squint but move forward, sniffing as I go. The wind whips my hair into my face, but within seconds, my eyes have adjusted and I'm able to get a good look around. Nothing. That's all there is anymore. Nothing.

After I've locked the door behind me, I hop on my bike and take off, pedaling around the house and moving to the road. Leaving the safety of my attic behind as I head down the street. With every pump of my legs, I'm surveying the road in front of me for signs of life or movement and inhaling through my nose. Long, slow breaths that make me feel like a hound dog but are necessary in this new world made of danger. If the dead are lurking nearby, their stink will give them away.

Before long the nearest neighborhood comes into view, but I pass it and keep moving east. Dad cleaned those houses out months ago, along with the next two neighborhoods. Which means I have three more miles to ride if I want to get someplace new. Taking the car would be nice, but I won't risk making any more noise than I already do.

When I reach a fork in the road, I veer to the left and pedal faster. The sun above me pounds down on the top of my head, making me wish I'd put on a hat, and my eyes are watering from the bright rays. Sunglasses would have been smart. Next time, I'll go out early in the morning, before it's too bright or too hot. A happy medium between the day and the night.

By the time I reach the outskirts of town, sweat is running down my back, and the thin fabric of my shirt is clinging to my stomach. I slow but don't stop, my eyes taking in every detail as I approach the town. Other than the branches swaying in the trees and the weeds—now up to my waist in a lot of areas—bending under the power of the wind, nothing moves. It's creepy how the world seems to have disappeared.

I pull into the driveway of the first house and hop off my bike under the shade of a tree. Using the toe of my shoe, I flick the kickstand down and move toward the trunk. Before I've made it all the way there, the rifle is in my hands, and by the time my back is leaning against the sturdy wood, I'm already studying the house. The front door is hanging open, but that's nothing new. The zombies that came back in the beginning eventually figured out how to let themselves out of their homes. I'd actually be more concerned if the front door was closed. It could mean someone went inside and shut the door behind them.

I count while I look everything over. When nothing moves, I do another quick scan of the area before charging across the yard toward the open front door. Inside, I move to the left and press my back against the wall, keeping my body flush with it as I head deeper into the house. My eyes move left and right so fast it's like I'm watching a game of ping-pong, but it's the only way to be sure there's nothing coming at me from either side.

Luckily, the house seems to be empty. Even better, the hall leads right into the kitchen. I only pause for a second when I step through the door before heading over to the opposite wall, once again putting my back to it. I take a deep breath through my nose, inhaling every ounce of dust floating through the air in search of the stink of decay, but turn up nothing.

When I exhale, I look around. A cabinet to my right is wide open, the contents spilling out onto the floor but still usable. Canned goods, boxed mac and cheese, pastas, soups, and even some boxes of cereal. Jackpot.

19

I take one quick look around before I kneel, twisting so my back is to the corner of the room and I'm facing the door I just came through. Then I slip my backpack off and start loading it with food, looking up between every can or box I grab so I can scan the kitchen.

I can't afford to let my guard down for even a second.

The bag is only half full when the pantry is empty, so I open a few more cabinets in search of more. Other than spices, though, I turn up nothing.

On to the next house.

I go back the way I came, retracing my steps to the front door. Keeping my back against the wall and my eyes moving so fast it starts to make me dizzy. Before stepping back out onto the porch, I scan the front yard. It's just as empty as it was when I went in, but that doesn't stop me from stepping to the other side of the door so I can get a better view.

Still nothing.

Back outside, I hurry across the yard and hop on my bike, panting and scanning the area. Breathing in through my nose as I pedal back out onto the road.

The next house isn't far, but I've barely made it past the yard I just left when a zombie stumbles out in front of me. Less than a second after the thing comes into view, the stink of rot slams into me.

I reach for my rifle without thinking, causing my bike to swerve and fall to its side. I jump, barely landing on my feet before stumbling forward a couple steps and eventually dropping to my knees. It doesn't matter, though, because I've already turned toward the thing shambling my way. Already have my rifle pointed at it as I scan the area for more.

There aren't any, at least not that I can see, and the one in front of me is still a good six feet off. It's a woman dressed in pajamas that were once pink but are now brown from dirt and probably dried blood. Black splotches dot the material, and the left pant leg is ripped from the knee to the ankle. It flaps behind her in the breeze as she stumbles toward me, grasping at the air and chomping her teeth like she's already chewing

20

on me.

Not if I have anything to say about it.

I sling the .22 over my shoulder as I get to my feet, pulling my knife in the process. If there were more of them I'd risk the gunshot, then get the hell out of here before a horde came running. But I can take just one.

The woman turns her head, and stringy brown hair flaps across her decaying face. Her eyes, milky and absent, seem to look through me. The vacant expression in her gaze will make the process of shoving my blade into her skull easier. If they looked more human, it would be tough.

When she's closer, I duck under her arms and twist around so I'm behind her. Unfortunately, the woman is about eight inches taller than my five foot one inches, which means I practically have to stand on the tips of my toes to reach her head. I've done it before, so it only takes a second longer to extend myself up to the right height and then slam the blade of my knife into the back of her head. Through her skull and deep into her brain.

Like a switch has been turned off, she drops to the ground. It's so sudden and so forceful that she takes my knife with her, and to get it back I have to get down on the ground and roll her body over.

The knife comes free when I tug, but before I get to my feet, I wipe the blade on the woman's pinkish pajamas. No sense taking the stink of zombie guts back home with me if I can avoid it.

I stand, scanning the area, but our little scuffle hasn't alerted any other zombies to my presence. Good. I'd like to get back home as soon as possible. The food I have on my back can last me a good two weeks with the rationing system I have down, and if the next house has even half as much, I should be good for a month.

Leaving the dead woman in the middle of the street feels wrong, but burying her would be a waste of time and effort, so I turn away from her and jog back to my bike. My gaze once again takes in the town, but just like before, it seems clear. Within seconds I'm back on my original course, pedaling down the road to the next house.

Just like I did with the first one, I park my bike under a tree and study the yard with my back pressed up against the trunk. This time, the front door is shut.

Skip it, or give it a shot?

I gnaw on my bottom lip while I think the whole thing through. Just because the door is shut doesn't mean someone is hiding inside. It could be that whoever lived here went somewhere else to die. Or never died at all. Maybe they headed out after the virus had taken its toll. It's possible they hopped in a car and drove to the coast where they could live out the rest of their life in a beach house.

It's what I think about doing sometimes.

I let out a deep breath through my mouth and then suck the air back in through my nose nice and slow. Just like before, it's clear. Fresh like a spring day. Which is exactly what it is.

I'm going for it.

Fast as a cheetah, I run across the yard to the front porch, then slam my back against the house. Gasping for breath, I twist my body so I'm able to look in through the front window. No furniture is overturned. Nothing broken or thrown across the floor. Nothing moving.

Looks clear.

I take a quick look over my shoulder before rapping my knuckles against the glass. Nothing happens, so I knock again, holding my breath as I wait. Still, nothing.

The house is empty.

At least I think it is.

With my heart pounding, I try the front door. To my shock—and fear—the knob turns. Whoever left this house didn't plan on ever coming back.

I slide my rifle off my shoulder as I step inside and press my back up against the wall. The house is cloaked in shadows, but it only takes two seconds to notice the pictures that have been removed. Above the couch three photos hang in a straight line, but there's a noticeable gap between the second and third one. The wall above the fireplace is empty too.

They took the pictures with them. Meaning the owners abandoned the house.

It helps ease my pounding heart, but I don't lower my gun as I move forward. Deliberately, keeping my eyes moving. Inhaling slowly. Pressing my back to the wall.

I make it to the end of the hall and do a quick survey of the area. To my right are the bedrooms, to the left the kitchen. I dart that way, rifle out, and slam my back against the refrigerator the second I'm in the kitchen. It's quiet and empty, but unlike the other house, no cabinets are wide open. I'm going to have to do some searching.

I start with the one closest to me and work my way around, looking over my shoulder every two seconds. My foot hits something, and I look down just as a bowl slams into the cabinets on the other side of the room, spilling moldy cat food all over the floor. I spin around, rifle ready, keeping my back against the cabinets as I wait to see if anything heard me. After a few seconds, I'm able to relax and go back to my search.

Halfway across the room, I hit the motherload. A cabinet crammed full of canned soup, vegetables, and fruit. It's like they were preparing for the zombie apocalypse.

There's no way I'll be able to fit it all into my bag. I could leave some and come back, or I could look for a second backpack. Which would mean going into the bedrooms.

The idea of searching the rest of the house makes me uneasy, but leaving it behind means risking someone else taking it. I could hide it, though. Put the cans I can't carry someplace that people wouldn't look.

But where?

I scan the kitchen and smile when my gaze lands on the refrigerator. Of course. No one in their right mind would open a refrigerator this far into the apocalypse. The electricity has been out for nearly nine months now, so anything in there isn't going to be salvageable.

I shove as many cans as I can into my bag and then zip it shut before turning to the disgusting task at hand. When I open the freezer, a stench fouler than anything I've ever encountered hits me in the face. I gag and step back, turning away as the protein bar I ate this morning jumps to my throat. But I can't afford to waste what little nutrition I have, so I swallow it back down. With everything I've seen and smelled since that damn virus killed most of the world, I should be able to handle the stink of rotten meat. No, I *can* handle the stink.

This time when I turn back, I hold my breath. Thankfully, the freezer isn't very full, and it only takes me a couple minutes to pull the contents out and dump them in the trash. Once that's done, I start piling cans into the useless freezer, breathing in and out through my mouth the entire time. And keeping a close eye on the door and the dining room behind me.

When I'm done, I shut the freezer and take a deep, cleansing breath. Not as cleansing as it should be since the rot I just took out of the freezer is now in the trashcan, but better at least.

With the canned goods hidden away and a backpack full of food to take home, I feel better about my chances of surviving. Hopefully Dad will be home in a day or two, and then we can get back on track. Maybe even head off to find our own beach house on the coast.

CHAPTER THREE

JIM

A zombie wraps its bony fingers around my neck, and I jerk back. My head slams into something soft. One of the dead? I twist to the left, but it's hard to tell. It's dark and hot. Suffocating. But I'm shivering. Cold and covered in goose bumps, while at the same time burning alive from the inside out. A constant throb radiates up my leg, and I look down to find a zombie gnawing on me.

I scream and kick, but he just digs his fingers in deeper, chewing on my leg as blood pours out like a river. When I kick a second time, the zombie lifts his head and turns to look at me. It's Jon. His face is rotten and distorted and one eye is missing, but I'd know that face anywhere.

"No. Jon. No!"

This time when I scream, it pounds against the inside of my head until I feel like my skull is being crushed. I pull my free leg back, then slam the heel of my shoe into Jon's face.

Over and over again until I'm free. I jump up, but I don't make it far. My head slams into something hard, and in seconds I'm back down, landing on top of a thousand bodies. Some dead, but most undead, and all of them stinking of rot and crawling with maggots. Black blood and rotten flesh cover me, and I thrash as I try to get away. It's impossible.

"Help." I don't even recognize my own voice. Maybe it wasn't me who said it. Maybe someone else yelled for help.

I look around, but all I can see is darkness, and when I reach out the walls surrounding me are solid. I twist until I'm sitting up and feel around. Within seconds, my fingers brush something smooth. A handle? I pull it and the door clicks. When I push it open, fresh air rushes in. I gasp, filling my lungs like I was on the brink of suffocating. The air is dusty, but it isn't thick with rot.

Where the hell am I?

I run my hands down my face and over my body. The scratchy surface covering me doesn't make sense. It's thick. Stiff. Barely allows me to move and makes it feel like something is trying to crush me. I pull at it, but it doesn't budge, and when I shift a pain so intense it nearly knocks the air out of me slams into my leg.

The cut. I remember now. I got cut and it's infected. And now I'm going to die.

I let out a deep breath, then refill my lungs with fresh air before lying back down. My head floats above my body, which aches from head to toe. Maybe death isn't such a bad idea. Everything here hurts, and with the way things are going, it isn't likely to get better any time soon.

Yeah. Death sounds nice.

I close my eyes and relax. The heaviness leaves my body, and the darkness that closes in is almost welcome.

CHAPTER FOUR

AMIRA

'm in such a rush to get my bike—and myself—back inside the garage that it almost doesn't register that the back door to the SUV is wide open. When it hits me I freeze, my hand still on the doorknob and the door open wide enough that anyone could come charging in.

Did I leave the door to the SUV open? Was it like that when I left?

I know the answer to both of those questions is no, but I can't help trying to think of a logical explanation that isn't *someone came inside and searched the car*. That would be the worst scenario I could face. It would leave me two choices: flee the only home I've ever known and try to find a new place to hide, or fight for my home. Both options feel like a death sentence.

I pull my knife while easing the door shut behind me, but I don't move right away. It's pitch black and I need to give my eyes a moment to adjust. While I wait, I press my back up against the wall and inhale slowly through my nose. Dirt. Dust. Oil and the faint scent of gasoline. All smells that I've always associated with the garage. No death or decay. Which is good. Still, there's something else. Something faint but present. I inhale again, and this time it's stronger. Mildew. Like something wet has been balled up and tossed in the corner to dry but never quite made it. Which doesn't make any sense. Other than my bike, I haven't disturbed anything on the first floor of the house since Dad left. Keeping everything in its place is important to my survival plan.

The darkness eases as my eyes adjust, and the outline of the car comes into view. As well as the open door. Nothing moves, not even when I take a small step forward. I pause, my gaze moving across the dark room, and then take another step before stopping again. Still nothing moves. But more importantly, nothing jumps out at me. Nothing tries to attack or kill me.

Maybe whoever came here left. Maybe they found what they wanted and left while I was gone.

I take another step. Pause and wait. Then take another. Pause and search the darkness for movement before stepping forward again. Every inch I get closer to the SUV, the stronger the mildew smell becomes. By the time I finally round the open door and look inside, my heart is moving faster than that damn roadrunner who was always getting chased by the coyote on Saturday mornings.

What I see doesn't make sense, so I hold still and wait for my eyes to adjust a little more. When they do, it still doesn't make sense.

It's a man. At least I think it is. He shifts, and I shuffle back while bringing my knife up, holding it in front of me. I expect him to jump at me and prepare myself to shove the blade into his chest if I have to, but he doesn't sit up. In fact, he doesn't move again. He just lies there.

I poke his leg with my free hand and then jerk back while I wait for him to respond. He still doesn't move.

Is he dead?

There's only one way to find out, and even though turning my flashlight on doesn't thrill me, I'm more than a little curious about who this man is and what he's doing in my mom's car.

I lower my backpack to the ground and pull my flashlight from the front pocket. Once the beam illuminates him, what I see makes even less sense than it did a few seconds ago. Silver lines of duct tape crisscross his body, holding what looks like strips of carpet to his torso, arms, and lower legs. It kind of reminds me of armor, and I almost laugh. It's like he's some modern day Don Quixote, covered in carpet armor as he heads off to fight windmills. Or zombies.

I poke him again, and this time when he shifts, I don't jump back. He still doesn't sit up, but he's moved just enough to allow me to get a good look at his face. His hair is so greasy it looks dark, but I'd be willing to bet that it's more blond than brown when it's clean. His face is covered in dirt and a scraggly beard, but what little skin is visible is pale and pink at the same time. Feverish and possibly a little sunburnt.

He's hurt, or maybe even sick. Maybe he needs my help...

But do I help him? That's the question. I've read enough books to know what happens at the end of the world, and I'm not dumb enough to think that I can fight off a full-grown man. I'd try, but I'd most definitely lose.

But just because he's a full-grown man doesn't mean I'd have to fight him off. Right? There have to be some good people left in the world. Dad and I saw what happened in the beginning, and even though most of the people left in the wake of virus went nuts, there were good people. We met some, even. This man could be one of the good ones. I could save him, and having him here could save me.

But how do I know if I can trust him?

I grab his leg and shake it, hoping to get his attention. When he turns his head his lips move, and his eyes open just enough to give me a good look at his icy blue irises. But they're closed again in seconds. He's not with it

29

enough for me to try to communicate with him right now.

I move the beam of my flashlight down, over his torso and the ridiculous carpet armor, then to his legs. That's when I see it. Blood. The left pant leg has been torn open at his thigh, and the little bit of fabric left is saturated with blood. Something black is wrapped around his thigh, probably to try and stop the bleeding. He could have an infection.

I have to get him inside. Get him healthy.

I slip my knife into its sheath and climb into the back of the SUV. Once there, the stink of mildew is so overwhelming that it makes my eyes water. I use my flashlight to get a good look at the man and notice several places where it seems like he attempted to cut through the duct tape. Maybe he was too out of it to cut himself free? Anything is possible.

That I can help him with.

I put my flashlight between my teeth and pull my knife back out. It doesn't take long to free his arms, and once the carpet falls away, I find the source of the stink. His clothes are damp under the carpet, which is also pretty wet. He either went for a swim or got caught in the rain. I'd guess the first one, though. It hasn't rained in over a week.

His lower legs are the next thing I work on, keeping a close eye on both him and the door at my back just to make sure no one sneaks up on me. The man twists a few times, and his mouth moves like he's trying to talk. I don't bother trying to figure out what he's saying, though. With as high as his fever is, it's probably just gibberish.

Getting the carpet off his torso takes a little longer, but when it finally falls away, I'm able to put my knife back in its sheath. He reeks—mildew, sweat, and filth—and he's going to need a change of clothes, but before I can take care of that I'm going to have to get him into the house. Which should be fun. Even sprawled out in the SUV he looks to be about ten inches taller than me.

I tuck my flashlight back in its pocket, then grab the man's arm and pull. He sits up pretty easily, but his head rolls like it's barely attached to his neck. I grab his shoulders to steady him, letting out a deep breath as I prepare myself for the challenge of getting this large man into my house.

I pull him with me as I back out of the car. He moves, and his eyes open a crack, but I get the sense he doesn't really know what's going on. Hopefully, he's able to stay upright.

My feet land on the garage floor, and I grit my teeth as I pull on the man's arm. He stumbles forward, slamming into me, and I have to wrap my arms around his torso to keep us both from crashing into the ground. The scent of sweat and mildew is so strong that I'm forced to breathe out of my mouth, but even that doesn't help get rid of the stink entirely.

I twist his body so we're side by side and his arm is over my shoulder, thankful that he seems to be holding up his own weight. He may be delirious from fever, but he's with it just enough to know that he's supposed to move, because when I walk he goes with me.

We make it to the door and I manage to get it unlocked while keeping us both upright, and then we're inside and moving down the hall. Until now, I hadn't considered where I was taking him, though. Getting him upstairs is out of the question, and dragging him up into the attic even more unlikely. Mom and Dad's room is on the first floor, but I haven't been inside it in months. Even though I don't love the idea, it's my only option and I know it.

We make it through the living room where his feet crash into the carefully spread-out Legos, sending them flying across the room. It gets even worse when we move through the kitchen. Forks and spoons slide across the floor and slam into the refrigerator, but somehow we manage to make it through without falling, which is the important part.

By the time we get to Mom and Dad's room, he's started to lean on me more, and I can tell his energy is almost spent. I make it inside and drag him to the bed, where he collapses face first, his body bouncing on the spring mattress. I'm panting from the effort of getting him here, but that doesn't stop me from flipping him over to make sure he's still breathing.

31

I press two fingers against his grimy neck, letting out a sigh of relief when his pulse thumps against my fingertips. It would have pissed me off if I'd dragged him all the way in here just to have to turn around and drag him back out.

Which brings me to another problem: he's obviously sick and in need of medication.

Unless he's been bitten.

Ice coats my veins, and I curse myself for being so stupid. Why hadn't I thought of that before? He could have been bitten and now he's going to turn into a zombie and I'm going to die, all because I dragged him into my house.

Shit. I should have checked him out before I brought him in!

I untie the black cloth—which turns out to be a scarf—and gingerly move the filthy fabric of his jeans aside. It isn't a bite, but it does look bad. Red lines go up and down his leg from the cut, and the skin surrounding the area is swollen and shiny. Hot to the touch. It's so inflamed that it looks ready to explode. He's bad off.

Still, he could have a bite somewhere else.

I get busy cutting off his clothes. Shirt first, which is so filthy and coated in sweat that it feels greasy against my fingers. When that's gone, I get his shoes off and work on cutting his pants from his body. The soiled clothes gets tossed into the corner to be disposed of later, but it only takes one look at the guy to realize I'm going to have to really clean him off. He's dirty from head to toe, and the only way to really see if he's been bitten—or scratched—is to wash him up.

Shit.

BY THE TIME I HAVE THE GUY CLEANED UP AND redressed, my cheeks are on fire. I'm no prude, but undressing and washing down an unconscious man, whether or not he's attractive, isn't comfortable. Add the fact that under all the soiled clothes and dirt, this man turned out to be very good-looking, and it makes for an extremely awkward time. I'm still blushing when I get him tucked firmly under the blankets, and even though he isn't awake, I'm thankful that it's nearly pitch black outside.

Before lighting a candle, I pull the curtains closed and toss a blanket over the window. Despite the awkwardness, I was able to look the guy over pretty well, and he wasn't bitten. The fever must be from the cut, which means he needs medicine. Lucky for him, I know just where to find it.

Dad's medicine cabinet is a goldmine of pill bottles. It's like every prescription he ever had filled was forgotten halfway through the regimen. It's a miracle he made it all the way to the zombie apocalypse without keeling over.

Why didn't he ever finish his prescriptions?

Maybe it was meant to be. Maybe that's why this guy found my house.

I roll my eyes at the ridiculous thought. Believing in fate after the zombie apocalypse has wiped out most of the world is like believing in Santa after a Christmas morning with no presents. Foolish and painful.

I separate the bottles into three categories. First, the ones that I know are antibiotics. Second, the ones I know are not. Third, the ones I don't have a clue about. The third category has the most bottles in it.

What kind of medicine was Dad on?

Blood pressure. That I know for sure.

Arthritis. That's another one. It got pretty bad last year right before he turned sixty.

Antihistamine? That one I'm not sure about, but it's possible. Everyone in my family had allergies except me, and being surrounded by cotton fields didn't help.

So what do I know about antibiotics? They're usually taken a couple times a day, which means I can rule out any of the pills whose labels say to take them once a day. What else? There usually aren't any refills. So, anything that has a refill is most certainly not an antibiotic.

Which leaves only two bottles in the unknown section and about six in the antibiotic pile.

I sort through the bottles of antibiotics and somehow manage to find two of the same drug. Even though they're a bit past their prime, they're our only option. Hopefully, they still have enough juice left in them to get this guy back on his feet.

It takes some doing to get him sitting up, but once I do, I manage to force a pill into his mouth and even get him to wash it down with a little bit of room-temperature apple juice. I don't want to waste the stuff, but since keeping him hydrated is as important as getting him medicine, I work to get him to swallow a little more before letting him lay back down.

He opens his eyes once his head is back on the pillow, but they're glazed over. Pretty, though. Very light blue and gentle. Hopefully the softness in those eyes is a sign that I made the right decision.

Bad thing is, there's no telling if I did. He could come to while I'm asleep and slit my throat, and I'd never even know it was coming. Shit. I really didn't think this through, which isn't like me at all. I analyze everything I do because I live in my head. Analyze it to death. That's what Dad always used to say, anyway. But this is uncharted territory. Tossing this guy out on his ass would be a death sentence for him, but bringing him inside could mean a very horrible end for me.

So what choice do I have now that he's in here?

I suck my bottom lip into my mouth and gnaw on it while I think it all through. Taking him back out now that I've wasted energy getting him cleaned up would be stupid. I could try to stay awake until I've had the chance to communicate with him, but with the fever raging in his body, that could be days from now. Lock him in here? Of course, the door locks from the inside. I could take the knob off. Maybe turn it around so I'm able to lock it from the other side. That might be the best option. If I can figure out how to do it, that is.

I take one last look at the guy passed out in my parents' bed before leaving the room. It isn't until I step into the kitchen that I remember the mess he made when I dragged him in. The silverware I had spread across the floor is now mostly gathered under the refrigerator, and the flour is smeared from the middle of the kitchen to Mom and Dad's room. There are even a couple really nice footprints going through it. Exactly the kind of thing I was trying to avoid. Change.

It only gets worse when I go out into the living room. The Legos are scattered across the room, the carefully planned-out pattern I'd created now nonexistent. That's something I'll have to change, but first I need to bring the food I gathered in from the garage and then get to work on the doorknob. The Legos will have to wait.

When I go into the garage, the first thing I do is shut the door to the SUV. I doubt it matters, but having things out of place unnerves me. I need the order to make me feel like I'm in control of this situation—which even I know is nuts. In a zombie apocalypse, no one is in control.

I park my bike and pan my flashlight around to make sure everything else is where it's supposed to be before dragging my backpack inside. Once there, the problem of where I'm going to stash the food hits me. The attic is where I feel safest, but with my new houseguest taking up residence in the master bedroom, it doesn't seem smart to be all the way up there. Staying down here means someone could sneak up on me, but going upstairs means this guy could die because he's too out of it to defend himself.

Since there are no right answers in this world, I do the logical thing and drag my backpack into Mom and Dad's room and stash the food in the closet. Right next to Mom's collection of designer purses. Michael Kors may have long ago turned into a zombie, but his handbags will live on for eternity.

I roll my eyes at my own stupidity.

With that taken care of, I get Dad's emergency toolbox and work on the doorknob. It's something I've never done, but all it takes is some careful observation and a flathead screwdriver. Ten minutes later I've created my own little jail cell, but I still don't feel totally comfortable, and installing a safety chain on the inside of the door doesn't seem to help either—locking this guy in is important, but so is being able to lock the rest of the world out of the room if I need to.

Standing in front of the bed, staring at the guy I just saved, I can't help feeling like a sitting duck. He could still come to while I'm asleep. Then what? I'd be dead. Or worse.

When a light bulb goes off in my head, I hurry out into the living room, jumping over the Legos spread out across the carpet. Michael's toy box sits in the corner, filled to the brim with the few items he hadn't yet outgrown. I dig through them, pushing the Nerf and cap guns aside until I find what I'm looking for. A pair of toy handcuffs. They're not heavy duty, but they are metal and they should be sturdy enough to keep this guy where he needs to be.

Back in the bedroom, I snap one end of the handcuffs around the guy's left wrist, being careful not to make it too tight, then attach the other side to the bedpost. The metal digs into his skin, which can't be comfortable, but having him secured makes me feel better.

Once I've cleaned everything up, it hits me just how exhausted I am. It has to be pretty late by now—close to midnight, I'd guess—and between the bike ride and saving this guy's life, I used up a lot more energy than normal today.

I drag a few blankets out of the hall closet and make myself a little bed in the corner of the room, putting my back against the wall so I'm able to see both the bed and the door. The dreaded .22 goes behind me, wedged between the wall and the blankets, and a knife gets tucked under my pillow. With the door locked and the guy as delirious as he is, I should be okay, but getting rest on the first floor is going to be tough after all these months of hiding out in the attic.

I know Dad had to go out and look for food, but I really wish he hadn't. If he were here, I'd feel better about this whole thing.

I sniff back the tears that try to force their way out. Grieving is something I haven't allowed myself to do. Partly because it's dangerous to lose control like that, but also because I haven't given up hope. Dad could still come back.

CHAPTER FIVE

JIM

The dream I'm trapped in feels oddly real at times.

A girl takes care of me, bringing me medicine and something sweet to drink that makes me feel like a kid again. She doesn't talk, but her brown eyes are so big and round that I feel like she can see inside me.

I can't move when I try, not that I want to. Every shift of my body causes pain to radiate up my leg. My muscles are sore from my head to my toes, and it feels like my brain is floating in a bucket of water.

Through it all, images from my past swirl around me. Mom. Becky. Even Rachel, who I haven't seen since she was six years old and disappeared into the system. Sometimes Jon's next to me, asking if I have his back as he turns to fire at zombies. The stink of death never goes away, and neither does the hot Georgia sun. Even when it's dark the damn thing scorches my skin, making my clothes stick to me.

I sleep, but never really rest. Every night is covered in darkness and pain and heat.

When the lights are on, I'm in and out. The girl feeds me, forces pills down my throat, and makes me sit up. She runs a cool, damp cloth across my forehead from time to time. There's always pain, though. No matter what she does, the throbbing never quite goes away.

"Who are you?" My words are so raspy they don't sound like me.

She blinks but doesn't answer. Maybe I never said the question out loud. My lips are so dry and stiff that I begin to wonder if I could move them.

"What's your name?" That time, I know I said it, but she still doesn't talk, so I close my eyes.

Maybe I'm losing my mind. It feels like it. Especially when the zombies show up, sinking their teeth into me. I scream and thrash, making the pain worse, and gentle hands shake my shoulders. The girl stands over me, her big eyes studying mine as she pats my arm. She doesn't seem real, so I blink, but when I open my eyes she's still there.

"I think I'm dying." I lay my head back down, sinking into a pillow so soft that it definitely can't be real. It threatens to swallow my body as the darkness once again closes in on me. So thick and heavy that I'm not sure I'll be able to make it back this time.

CHAPTER SIX

AMIRA

I am a nurse over the next couple days. The man drifts in and out, his lips moving at times, but most of his words making no sense. I barely leave his side. When he's awake, I give him juice or water and force pills into his mouth four times a day. On day two I even start feeding him some chicken broth from one of the cans of soup I found at the last house. I eat the noodles. When he tries to get up, I unlock the handcuffs and help him to the bathroom. Even though I've seen every inch of his body already, a flush of heat still shoots through me when I have to support him as he pees. But it's a good sign. It means he's staying hydrated. It means I'm doing a good job of keeping him alive.

Hopefully, it's worth it.

Having something to keep me occupied helps the time go faster and keeps my mind off how many days it's been since my father left. Until I found this man, I felt like I was counting every second of every day as it passed. Each tick of the clock was yet another reminder that Dad was gone for good. Now, though, I have other things to focus on.

On the seventh day after my father's disappearance, the man seems to really be able to focus on me for the first time. I bring him what will be his eighth dose of antibiotics, and he blinks as he looks me over, confusion and concern warring in his expression. He tries to sit, and when I help him, the handcuff pulls tight against the bedpost. The man glances toward his hand and shakes his head like he can't figure out what's going on. When he looks back at me, his blue eyes are more focused. More present.

It's odd. I've never seen someone so out of it from a fever.

When I hold the pill out, he opens his mouth willingly. I tuck the antibiotic inside, laying it right on his tongue, and the man surprises me a second time by taking the cup I'm holding. He gulps it down, holding my eyes the entire time, and a shiver moves through me. It isn't fear, though. More like excitement. Knowing that I'm finally going to be able to figure out where this man came from and who he is. That I won't be alone anymore. Even seven days is too long when there's no end in sight.

When he finally sets the cup down, his lips move. *"You saved me."*

I nod in response.

He frowns, and his eyes sweep over me before his lips move again. *"What's your name?"*

I let out a deep breath and shake my head. He doesn't seem to get it, because he repeats the question. He must still be too out of it to understand. I haven't tried to talk in months, though, and it isn't like I have a pen and paper handy. So, even though it's cliché and I hate doing it, I cover my ears and shake my head so he'll get it. The odds that this guy knows sign language are about a bazillion to one.

Understanding crosses his face, and his lips move again even though he now knows I can't hear him. *"Just my luck. I find someone who doesn't want to eat me, but I can't even communicate with them."*

He's talking to himself, so I pretend I don't understand. People who can hear do that a lot. Talk to themselves, I mean. I'm not sure why.

When he waves his hand in front of my face, I exhale again. I also roll my eyes so he'll know that I don't appreciate being treated like a dog.

He starts talking when he's sure he has my attention, and this time it's slower. More exaggerated. Even though it's irritating—like he thinks that just because I can't hear him my brain doesn't work as well as his—I have to admit it helps. He's still groggy from the fever, which makes it difficult to figure out what he's saying.

"Can you read lips?" I nod, and he mimics me as he wipes his hand across his sweaty face. *"How are you still alive?"*

I want to say, because you think I'm dumb, but since I'm still clinging to the promise I made to Dad, I just cross my arms and shove my bottom lip out in an exaggerated pout. It's the only way I can think to let him know that I'm unhappy about the implications of what he just said.

He shakes his head and shoves his free hand through his filthy hair. It flops across his forehead, so stuck together with dirt and grease that it's like a small tentacle. *"That's not what I mean."* He shakes his head again. *"Forget it. How old are you? Where are your parents?"*

He thinks I'm a kid. Again, I should be offended, but I'm not. I know I look young. I'm small and thin, and most people guess I'm fifteen or sixteen years old, so it's no surprise that this guy thinks the same thing.

I lift my hands, holding up all ten fingers. Then I lower them and do it again. The man's eyebrows shoot up when I lower them a third time, this time lifting only one finger.

"Twenty-one?" Doubt is written all over his face.

I just nod and point to him.

"I am twenty-six." Once again he says the words slowly, like he wants to make sure I'm getting everything he says. *"My name is Jim. What's your name?"*

43

Jim. I'm not sure what I'd imagined his name being, but that seems too common. Too simple. Over the last two days, I've studied every inch of his face, memorizing the lines that are hidden under his scraggly beard. He's handsome. Strong. Yet even in his fevered sleep he has a hardness about him that he can't hide, and he has scars on his body that emphasize the tough life he's lived.

Jim blinks, and I realize he's still waiting for me to tell him my name. I start to shape my fingers into the correct letters, but stop after the A. There's no point. Instead, I motion toward the nightstand and use my finger to draw the letters across the surface, cutting through the layers of dust that have collected there over the last several months.

A-M-I-R-A

When I'm finished I look up to find Jim nodding. Even though he hasn't acted threatening at all up to this point, it still shocks me when he extends his hand.

"Nice to meet you."

I only hesitate for a second before wrapping my fingers around his hand. His skin is cooler than it was, although still clammy, and the relief that rushes through me shocks me. This is the first conversation we've had, if you can even call it that, but it's nice. I hadn't realized how much I've missed having someone else to interact with.

Or maybe I hadn't allowed myself to think about it before now.

I can't help wondering where he came from and what he went through to get here. Both before and after the virus. Someone must have helped him tape that carpet to his body, which means he wasn't always alone. Who was he with before he passed out in my garage, and why did they get separated?

I wave my hand in the air, hoping he'll get the point and tell me a little more about himself. When he frowns, I blow out a frustrated breath so he'll know I'm as irritated as he is by the situation. Somewhere in the house is a dry erase board that we used to write groceries on, but it's been years since I

44

saw it. I'm not quite sure what Mom did with it.

Jim leans his head back and closes his eyes, and I take that as a hint. He's still getting over this infection and rest is important. If Dad had finished off those antibiotics, Jim might have died. We got lucky that my dad was so irresponsible, I guess.

When he shifts, his face contorts. He's probably in pain, but I can't ask him as long as I'm holding on to this damn promise to my dad. I know his bandage needs to be changed, but now that he's more with it, it's not as easy. For one, it's going to hurt like hell. For two, the cut is so high on his thigh that I can't just go for it without letting him know what I'm doing.

Damn. When I made that promise to Dad it seemed important, but it also didn't matter because we were able to communicate through sign language. I don't have that luxury now that he's gone, though.

Maybe it's time to rethink the whole thing.

CHAPTER SEVEN

JIM

When the bed shifts, I crack one eye and watch as the girl heads into the bathroom. She says she's twenty-one, but I don't believe it. I'd guess seventeen at he most. Not that I blame her for lying.

No matter how old she is, I'm damn lucky she decided to stick her neck out for me. If she hadn't, this thing would have killed me for sure. I've been here for days, in and out of consciousness. I don't even remember coming into the house, really. All I know is that when I woke up to find myself handcuffed to the bed and drenched in my own sweat, I was pretty sure I was hallucinating. If it hadn't been for the fact that I was tucked into a nice bed and wearing clean clothes, I would have freaked out. It took about two seconds to realize someone had washed me up, too.

The first time I spotted the girl, Amira, I was sure someone else was around to help her. She was asleep in the corner, a rifle lying across her lap. But no one else came. At some point I said hello, hoping to get her to wake up, but she didn't move. Now I know why. Deaf. Shit. How she made it this far is a mystery, but I can't wait to find out. She's gotta be tough, that's for damn sure.

The sound of drawers and cabinets being opened comes from the bathroom as I give the room I'm lying in a good once-over. The wall in front of me is practically wallpapered with framed pictures. A smiling couple whose hair changes from light brown to gray as the photos progress from one side of the room to the other, the images starting when they looked to be in their twenties and moving until they're well into their fifties. A little more than halfway across the room, a girl joins them in the pictures. Dark hair and a complexion that doesn't match that of her Caucasian parents. She's smiling in every one of them. Near the far wall, a second face starts showing up. A little boy with dark brown skin who is probably a good ten years younger than Amira.

They're happy pictures, which makes them depressing given the current state of the world. Amira is alone in the house, meaning everyone she loved was killed off either by the virus or the zombies. It's a story I've heard a million times, but one that hasn't gotten any less depressing with time. If the world can pull together and create a new society after all this loss, it will be a miracle.

Footsteps draw my attention away from the pictures, and I turn as Amira walks back into the room. She has a smile on her face, and it gets even bigger when she holds up a dry erase board. At first my cloudy brain doesn't know what the hell she's smiling about, but when she sits on the edge of the bed and starts to write, I let out a low chuckle.

After a few seconds, she turns the board to face me.

I FOUND THIS SO WE COULD TALK.

MY MOM AND BROTHER DIED FROM THE VIRUS, AND MY DAD LEFT A WEEK AGO TO FIND FOOD. HE HASN'T COME

BACK.

WHO ARE YOU?

Her dad disappeared just a week ago?

"Are you okay?" I want to reach out and touch her arm, comfort her in some way, but I hold back. For one, she doesn't know me, and it could be more threatening than comforting. For two, with my left wrist attached to the bed, it isn't exactly easy to move.

Amira nods and taps her marker against the question on the board.

Who am I? Shit. That's a loaded question if I've ever heard one. I've already given this girl my name and age, which is pretty much the bulk of what I tell people these days. Even Jon, who I'd venture to say was the closest friend I'd had in about ten years, didn't get much more than that. Yet this kid wants me to bare my soul like she's my shrink and I'm stretched out on some leather couch. Right.

I clear my throat like the sound of my voice matters and then say, "Jim. But I told you that already. I was headed to Atlanta with some people, but zombies surrounded the house we were hiding in. We were trapped, so I offered to lead them away. I cut myself trying to get the carpet off me and then got sick. Infection, I guess. Then I found your house."

Amira frowns and presses her lips together.

She said she can read lips, but now I'm not sure because she looks like she doesn't quite understand.

I open my mouth to ask her, but she isn't looking at me anymore. She's focused on the dry erase board, scribbling like crazy. When she's done, she flips it around so I can read it.

WHY DID THEY LET YOU SACRIFICE YOURSELF?

This girl doesn't miss a beat.

I shove my free hand through my hair, cringing at the greasy feeling it leaves behind on my skin. A bath would be nice.

"Well, one of the others volunteered first, but I couldn't

let her do that. It's a long story, really." I shake my head when I think about that group. Hopefully, they made it to Atlanta. There haven't been a whole lot of people who gave me hope that humanity would hold on, but that group was one. "They had a new baby. Brand new. I had to make sure they got her to safety. Plus, one of the men in the group was immune. That's why we were going to Atlanta in the first place, so the CDC could use his blood to create a vaccine."

Amira sits up straighter and her brown eyes grow to twice their size, seeming to take up most of her face. She starts to move her hands but then shakes her head and gets busy writing. Sign language, of course. I've never met a deaf person before, but knowing how to communicate with one right now would be handy.

When she's done writing, she holds the board up again.

THE CDC? PEOPLE ARE STILL THERE? AND SOMEONE CAN BE IMMUNE TO THIS THING?

"That's right." I nod as I say it. "We were as surprised as you. I was in Colorado, living in a town that was all cleared out. When we got in touch with the CDC, it gave us hope. Then we found this guy who was immune and it only made sense to get him there. They think they can create a vaccine, but I don't know much about that."

I shrug. Truth is, I don't know much about anything. Not that I want her to know that. She doesn't need to know that I was a screw-up who barely made it out of high school before this, or that I spent the last few years in prison.

Amira nods slowly, thinking it all through. The wheels in her head are spinning, but the last thing I want is more questions, so I toss one at her instead.

"What happened to your dad?" She isn't looking at me, so I touch her arm to get her attention and repeat the question.

She starts scribbling again, and I lean back and shut my eyes. My head is better—about a million times clearer, actually—but I still feel like a truck hit me. It's going to take a while to get my energy back.

The soft brush of Amira's fingers against my arm brings me back to the present, and I crack one eye.

WE WERE ALONE FOR MONTHS. HIDING IN THE HOUSE. HE WENT OUT TO FIND SUPPLIES. IT WAS ONLY A WEEK AGO. HE'LL BE BACK. I'VE BEEN HIDING IN THE ATTIC, BUT I HAD TO COME DOWN BECAUSE I RAN OUT OF FOOD AND WATER.

He'll be back? She's kidding herself, I think, but I'm not going to be the one to rain on her parade.

Instead I say, "I know you aren't going to like me saying this, but it's a miracle you made it." Amira scowls, and I find myself chuckling. She's a spunky little thing. "Sorry, but it's true. I can't imagine not being able to hear when a zombie sneaks up on me."

Amira goes back to writing on her board.

I HAVE A FEW TRICKS THAT HELP ME.

"Smart." I give her a nod of approval. "You're smart. You'd have to be to make it this far. Whether or not you can hear."

She sits up straighter and smiles, and something about it makes her look older. She's short, probably not much taller than five feet, and thin. But under the loose-fitting shirt and shorts she has curves, and her legs are shapely. Long, despite her short stature and toned. Her big brown eyes seem innocent until that attitude sneaks out, which in itself makes her seem older.

She said she was twenty-one.... Maybe she wasn't lying?

"How old are you, really?" I ask, narrowing my eyes on her face.

Amira gives me an exaggerated frown before writing on her board, and just like that I'm laughing again.

21!!!

The way she underlined the number and added three big exclamation points makes me laugh so hard that my throat tickles, and then I start coughing. I bend over and hack and cough until my throat is raw and my head is pounding. The handcuff clangs against the bedpost and the metal digs into my flesh. I try not to pull on it too hard, but by the time I'm done, the skin on my wrist is raw. When I finally get myself pulled together, I look up to find Amira standing in front of me with a glass of water. She's like my own little nurse.

"Thanks," I say and then clear my throat.

I gulp the water down and hand the glass back to Amira, who sets it on the nightstand. She motions for me to lie down, and I obey. Mainly because just that little bit of activity has worn me out. Sleep sounds good. I need to get my energy up so I can pay this girl back by taking her to Atlanta. After everything she's done for me, she deserves it.

She doesn't give me a chance to relax, though. The second I'm flat on my back, she pulls the covers down, and when her hands brush against my thigh—seriously close to my dick—I bolt upright.

I grab her hands. "What are you doing?"

She shakes her head and pulls her hands from my grasp, waving toward my crotch.

Did I just enter some kind of alternate reality where it's normal for nurses to jack you off?

It's been so long since I had sex that just thinking about it makes all the blood in my body redirect itself to my crotch. Oh, hell no. I grab the covers with my free hand and pull them back up. This girl says she's twenty-one, but she could be fifteen for all I know, and that is not about to happen.

Amira shakes her head and grabs for the blanket, but I hold on tight.

"We're good. You don't have to do that."

She rolls her eyes and blows out a breath so hard that it moves her dark hair off her forehead. Then she scoops up her little dry erase board and goes back to writing.

When she flips it around, I almost laugh. Shit, I'm dumb

as fuck.

I NEED TO CLEAN YOUR CUT AND GET YOU FRESH BANDAGES.

"Damn." I shake my head, and this time when she reaches for the covers, I don't stop her. "Sorry."

She isn't looking at me, so she most likely missed my apology, but it makes me feel better to say it at least. Leave it to me to assume she was going for my goods.

It isn't until she's pulling the bandage away from my throbbing leg that it hits me, though. She's already seen my goods. When I crawled into the backseat of that SUV I was wearing jeans, and under those a pair of boxers. Now I'm in shorts. On top of that, I'm pretty clean, meaning she must have washed me down when she changed me. Just thinking about Amira changing my clothes and cleaning me up gets my blood pumping even faster than before, and it's all directed at one part of my body.

I'm not a kid, and I don't get embarrassed easily, but when Amira takes a step away from the tent that has now pitched itself in my shorts, heat spreads across my face. There's a part of me that wants to tell her it's out of my control and has nothing to do with her, but that would be a damn lie. She's a pretty little thing. I just hope to God she really is twenty-one like she claims she is. If I turn out to be a dirty old man on top of a convict and an asshole, I'd say I've pretty much run out of redeeming qualities.

Amira doesn't meet my gaze, but I don't miss the flush in her cheeks when she starts writing on her board again. She hands it to me before turning away, obviously trying to avoid looking me in the eye.

I'M GOING TO GET SUPPLIES. ARE YOU IN PAIN? I HAVE PILLS.

I write *no* on the board so I don't have to embarrass her any more than I already have, then lay my head back and close my eyes. I'm beat, but it's mostly to save her from embarrassment. Things down south haven't changed, and

53

with the anticipation of having her soft hands on me, it's not likely to happen any time soon. She'll probably appreciate it if I pretend to be asleep.

The sound of her soft footsteps moves across the room, and I have fight to keep my eyes closed. Having her here is nice, and seeing her is reassuring. After the delirious dreams of the past couple days, I like knowing that I'm not alone. That someone gentle and kind is here with me.

The bed dips when she sits down, but just barely—she's so small she can't weigh more than ninety pounds soaking wet—and a couple seconds later she runs a damp cloth over the cut. Air hisses through my teeth when a sting spreads across my thigh, and I let out a deep breath.

When I open my eyes, I find her watching me.

She gives me a sympathetic smile, then turns back to the cut. Every time she touches it more pain spreads through me, and by the time she's done, my hands are clenched into fists.

The board is still lying on my stomach when Amira uses the palm of her hand to wipe the letters away and writes one word across the clean surface.

SORRY.

I force out a smile, which she returns, and just like that, all the discomfort of a few minutes ago is gone.

"I'm going to get some rest," I say as she gathers the first aid stuff. I take a chance and hold up my arm, which doesn't make it far, thanks to the handcuff. "You think you can take this off now? I promise to be good."

The smile I give her is sincere, but hesitant at the same time. I don't want to freak her out, but sleeping would be a lot easier if I wasn't chained to the bed.

She holds my gaze for a few seconds before nodding, and when she produces a key from her pocket, I let out a deep breath. She doesn't look my way when she unlocks the cuffs. The metal falls away and I let out a deep breath, rubbing the raw skin on my wrist. The corner of Amira's mouth tips up, but she doesn't meet my gaze before turning away.

CHAPTER EIGHT

AMIRA

I've lived in a world of silence most of my life, but this new world is different. The silence that has settled over everything is different. Absolute. Terrifying.

Jim sleeps while I lean against the wall by the door, my .22 in my lap. Staring at the bedroom door. If I were safely tucked away in my attic, I'd read. But I can't do that here. I can't even relax down here, really. All I can do is focus on the door like I'm waiting for something to happen, but I'm not sure what I'm waiting for. My dad? Zombies? Someone even more terrifying? It's impossible to know.

I've barely slept since I brought Jim into the house. Every time I start to nod off, I jerk awake, thinking someone or something is standing over me. They could sneak up on me down here. Could break a window and come inside. I'd never hear it. If I take my eyes off the door for even a second, it could be the end of me.

I didn't make it this far to die now.

My gaze moves from the door to Jim long enough to see that he's still asleep, and then I'm watching the door again. Bringing him here was a good idea. I can trust him. He can help me. Make things easier when I go out to look for supplies. He can watch my back.

He was worth the risk I took.

I jerk awake so violently that my head bangs against the wall and the .22 drops to the floor. My right hand grabs the rifle while my left hand massages the back of my skull, but my eyes are on the bed. Which is currently empty.

Shit. Maybe I shouldn't have taken the cuffs off him yet...

Even though I don't think Jim is threatening, my heart is still pounding like crazy when I haul myself to my feet. He's been in bed for days, so it makes sense that he'd want to get up and move around. And that he wouldn't want to disturb me.

That's all it is. He's stretching his legs.

I peek into the bathroom even though it's dark and I'm ninety-nine percent sure it's empty. It is, so I head out into the kitchen. Also empty. After dragging Jim in from the garage I cleaned up the flour, making it once again look like an accidental spill. Now, though, there are footprints in the white powder. I need to tell this guy not to walk through my warning system.

The living room is empty, and for some reason the Legos that I had taken the time to rearrange have been picked up. I stare at the now-filled bucket, blinking like if I look at it long enough it will spill over and all the blocks will go back to where I left them. When it doesn't happen, I head into the family room.

It's also empty, but the front door is wide open. Air that's sticky and warm blows in, sweeping through the house. Even though it's nice—it's warm from the spring sunshine, but not yet overwhelmingly humid—it causes a million horrible scenarios to flip through my head in a matter of seconds. All of which start with Jim being torn to pieces and end with me

56

as a zombie.

I pull the rifle off my back as I rush outside, pointing it in front of me. Totally willing and ready to fire if necessary. The sun nearly burns my corneas when I step out, but even before I've shielded my eyes, I catch sight of Jim. It isn't until I've blocked the bright rays that I realize what he's doing.

He's just sitting on the porch. Or, more accurately, lounging on the outdoor rocker and smoking a cigarette. I lower my gun when he shoots me a smile. He nods toward the chair at his side, and without thinking, I sink into it. Being out in the open like this, sitting on my front porch as if the world hasn't gone to shit, is surreal. Probably the most surreal thing I've done since the apocalypse started.

Jim holds a pack of cigarettes up. *"Found these in the house. I hope it's okay."*

I nod.

They're Dad's, but I can't tell Jim that because I left the damn dry erase board in the house and I haven't yet given up on my promise. Like if I do, it will mean Dad is gone for good. Without the board, I can't tell Jim anything. Which means I might as well be alone again.

I could just go inside and get the board.

I start to get to my feet, but Jim grabs my arm. *"Stay."*

Using my pointer finger, I pantomime writing, then point to the house so he'll understand.

He shakes his head. *"We should learn to communicate without it. I can ask you yes and no questions. Right?"*

That will sure as hell limit what we can talk about. Then again, maybe that's part of his plan. When I asked him who he was, he didn't give me a whole lot of information, and nothing about who he was before the virus.

I narrow my eyes on Jim's face, giving him a good once-over. He looks comfortable holding the cigarette, which means he was a smoker before. I've seen him naked, so I know he has a bunch of tattoos. His right arm is covered in ink that starts at his elbow and goes up to his shoulder, he has another big one on his left arm, and one on his back

57

across his left shoulder blade, as well as one on the right side of his chest. All of them are huge, except the one on his chest, which is so small and delicate that I had to lean forward to read it. It's just three numbers: 11 14 10. A date, I'm assuming, but what it means, I don't have a clue.

His facial hair is more than just stubble, telling me it isn't a recent addition, and his hair is longer than average too. He's young, but the scars on his back and arms — they're too old to be from the apocalypse — say he's had a rough life. Despite all that, he's good-looking and confident, but not in a cocky way, and very guarded. Even how he's sitting now, turned toward me but not completely. Watching me, but out of the corner of his eye. Doing everything he can to seem like he isn't interested while at the same time never letting me out of his sight.

"Do you want to talk?" He shifts so he's facing me a little more, but his upper body is still turned the other way.

Instead of responding, I reach for the cigarettes, my eyes on him.

Jim pulls the pack away. *"I don't want to contribute to the delinquency of a minor."*

I roll my eyes, and my hands move on their own, signing.

Jim's fingers wrap around my right hand, and my left one falls to my lap. Useless. Just like the signs are.

This is stupid.

"Sorry," I say, working hard to form the word.

Jim's blue eyes get huge, and he releases my hand. *"You can talk?"*

I spread the fingers on my right hand, tilting them from side to side. "I haven't done it in a long time." Not since the zombies. After they showed up, Dad decided sign language was the best thing. To Jim, I say, "Without the ability to hear, I don't know how loud my voice is, or how far it carries. I don't know when there's something lurking around the corner. My dad made me promise not to talk anymore. He wanted to keep me safe."

Before he disappeared, my dad made it his mission to

help me get lost in my world of silence. He helped me understand what things made noise and what didn't. I learned how to make my movements as small as possible and how to control my breathing so it wouldn't alert anyone to my presence. Now, looking back, I think he realized he wasn't always going to be around to keep me safe. And that hurts. Knowing he prepared me to survive on my own.

Jim is nodding when he puts his cigarette between his lips. He inhales slowly, his eyes on me like he's thinking something through. When he talks again, smoke comes out with the words, making it difficult for me to really grab hold of them.

"...*makes sense...*"

I shake my head and grab his chin, his wiry facial hair scratchy against my fingers, and turn his face toward me. "Again."

"*I said, that makes sense. These days it would be handy for everyone in this world to know sign language.*"

He's right, but I'm not about to set up a class at the local community college.

When I realize I'm still holding his chin, I let it go. My hand falls into my lap, and the sigh I let out is so big it causes me to take a look around. Until now, I'd actually forgotten that we were sitting outside. In the open. It's been months since I've been this relaxed, and it's nice. Knowing someone else is here to back me up.

I hold my hand out and nod at the pack of cigarettes.

This time, Jim grins and pulls one out. "*Promise you're over eighteen?*"

I roll my eyes, and he chuckles.

When I take the cigarette from him, his blue eyes twinkle like he's a twelve-year-old about to play a prank on someone.

I narrow my eyes. "What?"

He shakes his head and chuckles again, his shoulders trembling with the silent laughter.

"Just light it." I plop the cigarette between my lips.

When Jim flicks his thumb over the lighter, it sparks but doesn't catch. He does it a second time, this time cupping his free hand around it to keep the wind at bay. The flame catches, and I lean forward so I can light the cigarette, inhaling slowly to help it along. It does, and the grimy flavor of smoke and tobacco fills my mouth. It moves down my throat, scratching at my insides like it has nails, then makes its way into my lungs. The smoke burns when it settles there, and when I exhale it tickles my insides. Of course, I cough. Not a little ladylike cough, either. A big cough that probably makes me look like I'm trying to hack up a lung.

When I look up, Jim is laughing his head off.

I press my lips together, both to let him know that I'm pissed and to keep the cigarette from falling into my lap, and then shove him so hard he nearly tumbles out of the chair. He catches himself just before he falls, and even though his back is to me, I can tell he's still laughing because his shoulders are shaking like crazy.

What a jerk!

I pluck the cigarette from my mouth and say, "I should have tossed your ass out of my garage and let the zombies eat you."

Jim's lips are moving when he finally turns his head, and once again I'm forced to grab his chin and turn his face toward mine.

"Slower. Look at me when you talk."

He gives me a nod that is so exaggerated I have the urge to slap him upside the head, and when his lips move again, that urge only grows. *"Okay. I will make sure I look right at you next time I call you a child."*

"I'm not a child." I scowl and take another puff from the cigarette, this time managing to swallow the smoke down without coming close to dying.

"Have you ever smoked before?" Jim's eyebrows are so high that they're lost under his greasy hair.

"Once. When I was in high school. I had a friend over and we found my dad's cigarettes." A smile tugs at my lips when I

60

think about it. "He hid them from Mom, even though she knew he smoked. Said he liked to have something private in his life. My friend and I found them tucked inside his toolbox, and we smoked one behind the garage. When my parents found out I was grounded for a week. I never did it again."

Jim's shoulders shake harder. *"Or anything else rebellious, I bet."*

"Unlike you." I point the cigarette at him. "I bet you've tried everything in the book."

A shadow falls across Jim's face, and the smirk he shoots me isn't as open as it was a few seconds ago. *"I wrote my own book."*

I'm not surprised.

"What did —"

Jim tosses his cigarette to the ground as he jumps to his feet, grabbing the .22 from my lap so fast that I jerk back and my chair wobbles. I try to stop it from toppling over, but I don't succeed. In the blink of an eye, I'm on my ass and Jim is charging across the porch. Practically dragging his bad leg behind him. I can see the side of his face when his lips move, but it isn't turned toward me enough to allow me to read his lips. Is he talking to me, or is someone else around?

I jump to my feet and twist to face Jim. He has the rifle raised, but whatever he's aiming at isn't in sight. I take a deep breath in through my nose as I pull out my knife, sucking in as much air as I can, but as far as I can tell, it's clear. Either the zombie is upwind, or it's not one of the dead.

A shiver shoots through me. Sometimes, people are even worse.

I rush across the porch, but Jim steps in front of me before I can make it to his side. That doesn't stop me from peeking around him, and when I catch sight of two men standing in the yard, my hand tightens on my knife.

Jim's lips are moving when I look up, but from this angle I don't know what the hell he's saying. Based on how tense his body is, though, I'd guess he isn't asking them to come inside and join us for a cup of coffee.

CHAPTER NINE

JIM

"Don't come a step closer!" My voice booms across the open space, but the men don't even flinch. I'm not a threat to them, which means they *are* most definitely a threat to me. "I won't hesitate to shoot."

"We're not looking for trouble," the taller of the two says, lifting his hands just an inch. He's probably in his forties, but his thick beard and leathery, sun-scorched skin makes him look older. "Just passing through."

His dark eyes move past me to where Amira is standing, and I step closer to her.

Shit. I got too comfortable out here. Forgot that it was all on me to keep a lookout. It's been a long time since I've been on my own, and I'm not used to it. I'm used to going into buildings with Jon at my side, knowing he has my back the whole time. We were a team. Moved as one and kept our eyes and ears open for trouble every step of the way. It isn't like that with Amira. Can't be like that. I have to be her ears.

The other man, the shorter of the two, takes a step forward, and I don't miss it when he slips his hand into the pocket of his dark trench coat. "We're not here to hurt you."

He smiles, which I think is supposed to calm me down, but all it does is make every hair on my body stand on end. Unlike the first one, this guy has no beard, meaning I can see every muscle that twitches in his face when he looks us over.

"Bullshit." I move my finger to the trigger. "I want you to pull your hand out of that pocket real slow. Understand? Nice and easy. Like your life depends on it."

The man nods, but before he moves he glances at his partner. Just like the shorter one, the other guy is wearing a dark trench coat. It's way too hot for this guy to be wearing a jacket like that. Anything could be hidden in there, and my imagination is running wild with the possibilities.

"Slowly," I say.

The shorter man takes my advice and pulls his hand out of his pocket slowly, but I'm not dumb enough to let my guard down. When it's finally out his fingers are curled around something, and he smiles. Whatever it is, it's orange. I shift, hoping to get a better look, but I don't lower my gun. It's an actual orange. A big one.

Maybe he isn't here to —

Something scrapes against the porch at my back, and I spin around so fast that I knock Amira to the ground. A man rushes toward me, knife raised, but before he can get halfway I pull the trigger. The crack of the gunshot echoes through the air, leaving a ringing sound behind in my ears. I spin back around to find the other two men charging across the yard. The taller man is so close that I couldn't fire again even if I had another bullet, so I swing the rifle around and slam the butt of the gun into his head instead. He goes down with a grunt, but the other man is right behind him.

"Ammo!" I yell before I remember that Amira can't hear a damn word I say.

64

Not that it matters. The short guy is too close to give me a chance to reload, anyway.

Just like with his friend, I use the gun to my advantage, slamming the butt into the man's stomach so hard that I actually hear it when all the air whooshes from his lungs. He doubles over, and I take the opportunity to slam the stock into his face. Blood sprays from his nose and he groans, but I've already turned my attention to the other guy. He's down, but not out. Luckily, I grabbed a knife before coming outside to smoke. I toss the rifle aside and have my knife out before it even hits the ground, and two seconds later, the tall man is choking on his own blood. I pull the knife from his neck and give the second man the same treatment.

That's when I remember Amira. In the middle of the scuffle, I'd forgotten all about her. Thankfully, I spin around to discover that she's a hell of a lot more capable than she looks. The man I shot is on the porch, blood pooled under his body from the wound and even more coming from the slice Amira made across his throat.

I drop to my knees at her side, letting out a deep breath when pain pulses up my thigh, but her eyes are so focused on the man in front of her that she doesn't notice. Even when I touch her arm, she doesn't look away. With the way she's staring at the cut in the guy's neck, I'd bet my life that this is the first time she's had to kill a living, breathing person.

"Hey," I say even though I know she can't hear me. I touch her arm again, and this time she turns to face me. "Are you okay?"

She nods, and her lips move a little before words finally come out. "I think so."

"Not hurt?"

She shakes her head.

"Good." I run my hand down her arm, hoping to calm her. "That's good. We got lucky."

Her eyes move back to the body in front of her. "I knew my luck would eventually run out." She looks back at me. "If you weren't here, I would have died."

65

I open my mouth to tell her she did a good job, but when she throws herself against me, there's no point. She's not looking at me, so the words would be wasted. Plus, with her tiny body pressed against mine, the weight of what could have happened hits me like a ton of bricks. She could have been killed — or worse — and it would have been my fault.

Her arms tighten around my neck, and before I can talk myself out of it, I'm hugging her back. It feels wrong because we just met, but I can't deny the overwhelming desire to protect her that's been building inside me since the moment I learned she was alone. It's like a throbbing in my chest, making me want to hold her closer. Tighter. Maybe even never let her go.

After a few seconds, I force my arms to drop and untangle hers from around my neck. She's still looking at the body, so I have to physically grab her chin and force her eyes on me.

"I need bullets. Tell me you have more." She nods. "Good. Let's get them. Then I'm going to have to get the bodies out of here. I want you to be the lookout while I do that. Okay?"

She nods again, then gets to her feet.

I don't follow her inside but instead get busy searching the pockets of the men who died by my hands. Their trench coats turn out to be nothing more than a smoke show. They're long enough to make the people around them think they have dozens of weapons hidden beneath the folds, while concealing literally nothing but one knife each. They don't have a scrap of food other than that orange. Which is odd, considering the fact that these men are not thin. They're sturdy, and they were fast when they charged us. They weren't starving, and they weren't weak from exhaustion.

Either they have a place not too far from here, which means there could be more, or they've been traveling. Moving from place to place. Killing people as they go and taking what little they have.

Gingerly, trying to disturb my wound as little as possible, I get to my feet when Amira walks back out onto the porch.

The box of bullets she holds out is big enough to make me feel a little more secure about our situation, but not a lot, considering a .22 doesn't have a whole lot of power.

"Do you have more?"

"Two boxes in the attic."

Thank God.

"Good." Even though it's stupid and a waste, I keep my voice level and my concern tucked away inside. She doesn't need to know I'm worried about more men coming. "I'm going to drag the bodies to the edge of the field. Can you watch my back?" Amira nods, but handing my life to her without making sure she knows what she's doing would be dumb as shit. "You can shoot that. Right?"

She rolls her eyes so far back that only the whites are visible. "Fuck you."

A laugh rips its way out of me that helps ease some of the tension in my chest. "Watch it or I'll wash your mouth out with soap."

She sticks her tongue out, and I chuckle again. Something about her makes me feel like a teenager all over again, only this time I'm not a little prick who's trying as hard as he can to fuck up his life. Just the opposite. I'm trying to do right by myself and by someone else. Can't really say I've ever been in this situation before. At least not successfully.

My thigh throbs when I drag the smaller of the three guys off the porch—the one Amira killed—and even though I don't have to look over my shoulder to make sure she's doing her job, I do. She has the rifle held so firmly in her hands that she reminds me of a soldier, and her eyes never stop moving. Never stop scanning the distance. It's like watching a tennis tournament, the way her eyes bounce back and forth. She also has her back up against the house so nothing can come up behind her. Smart. No wonder she's still alive.

By the time I reach the edge of the field, I'm sweating my ass off and my leg is screaming for relief. I haven't had a shower since we left Hope Springs, which was probably a good week ago—maybe longer—and I have without a doubt started to smell like ass. I wipe the sweat off my forehead as I trudge back toward the house, ignoring the throbbing in my leg and the ache in my limbs that tells me I am not completely over this fever yet. Crawling into bed sounds nice, but I have two more bodies to pull away. Shit.

I pass Amira, heading for the other two bodies, and she nods. Her footsteps scrape quietly against the porch at my back. Her dad did a helluva job teaching her to be silent, and it couldn't have been easy. Just thinking about all the little things we do on a daily basis and the noises they make—sounds she has no way of knowing exist—blows my mind. Yet here she is, walking behind me and making no more noise than a fly buzzing by my head. It's a skill even a lot of hearing people don't possess.

I grab the next guy, the first one I killed, and start to drag him off the porch when Amira touches my arm.

"What are you doing?" she asks.

It's not her fault, but it still irritates the hell out of me when I have to drop his arms and turn to face her. I'm ready to be done with this so I can get some rest, and I'm not sure how much longer this damn leg is going to hold me up. Having to look at her every time I talk is a pain in the ass.

"I'm taking him to the opposite side of the yard." I wipe sweat off my forehead and use the break to give my bad leg a rest, shifting most of my weight to the other leg. "I want to spread out the bodies. Once they start to rot, the smell could deter people from coming this way."

She frowns and shakes her head so hard that her dark hair swishes around her shoulders. "No. The smell helps me know if there are zombies around. I depend on my sense of smell more than you because I can't hear."

She signs as she talks, and I try to file the motions away for later, hoping to absorb some of the sign language so communication with her is easier. My brain, however, is way too muddled for that right now.

I'm also too beat to have a debate with her.

"This is what I'm doing."

I turn away before she can argue, but once again she grabs my arm. When I don't look at her, she steps in front of me, putting herself between me and the body.

"This is how I survive!" Her hands move so quickly that I have to take a step back.

I lift mine like I'm trying to stop her from punching me. "Calm down. It's going to be okay. You have me now. I can be your ears."

She freezes. Blinks. Then stares at me for a few seconds like she's trying to decide what to say. All I can do is stare back and try to figure out why what I said would make her look at me like that.

"What?" I finally ask.

"Thinking." She shakes her head and looks down at the bodies, then across the yard. Finally, she nods. "Okay."

Since she isn't looking at me and the throbbing in my leg has gotten increasingly persistent over the last few minutes, I don't ask for an explanation of exactly what she's thinking. I just turn back to the body and drag it off the porch toward the other end of the yard.

Just like before, Amira stays by the house and keeps an eye on the surrounding area. It's pretty flat, with nothing more than green fields separating us from the woods in the distance. If something were to head our way, it would be difficult for it to take us by surprise.

When I go back for the last body, Amira doesn't stop me. I have to drag it further away than the other two, and by the time I've made it all the way past the backyard to the edge of the field, I'm gasping for breath. My legs are unsteady and weak, like those damn pieces of wet carpet are once again taped to them, and the throbbing in my thigh has gotten so bad that pain has begun to pulsate through the rest of me as well.

I'm done, though. Now all I have to do is get back inside. Then I can lay down and get some rest.

Halfway back to the house my knees buckle and my legs give out, and I slam into the ground. Somewhere in the distance, Amira makes a sound that might be a word, but I'm not sure because my brain isn't exactly working. Footsteps head my way, and I try to get up. Try to use my hands to push my body off the ground. It doesn't work, though, and all I end up doing is falling face first into the grass.

"Jim?" Amira drops to the ground at my side.

"That's the first time you've said my name." My face is pressed against the grass, so I roll onto my back, groaning at the effort it takes. Amira hovers above me, her forehead creased with worry and her dark hair falling into her face. She pushes it aside as she looks me over, but I grab her chin in my hand and force her to look at me. "I like hearing you say my name."

A flush spreads across her cheeks just before my hand drops to my side and darkness creeps across my vision.

CHAPTER TEN

AMIRA

Round two of getting Jim into the house is going to be even harder than round one was. Last time he was delirious but conscious, so he was able to help me out a little. This time, however, he's out cold.

I slap his cheeks a couple times—not too hard, but hard enough to hopefully get his attention. His lips don't move, so I try again. Still nothing.

I exhale and look around.

We're out in the open, and if these guys have friends, it could be trouble. Something about the expression on Jim's face after he searched the bodies made me think he was concerned. Which means I should be even more worried. Shit.

I have to get him inside, and fast.

When I slap him again, I put more effort into it. "Jim," I say, hoping to rouse him.

My face is still hot from what he said, but I don't know why. Why would he care if I say his name? And why would knowing that he cares send a shiver of warmth shooting through me? Neither are questions I have answers to, but even worse, I don't have time to think about it right now.

After what feels like the hundredth slap, Jim's eyelids flutter. The icy pools behind them are hazy and unfocused, but he moves his head. And his lips. Whatever he's saying, though, is nothing but gibberish. At least to me.

"Jim," I say again.

Using my words after all this time doesn't feel right, especially out in the open like this, but it made Jim too happy for me to even consider stopping. Plus, I always liked being able to talk to another person. It was like having a real connection with the hearing world.

This time when Jim's eyes open, his lips move slowly enough that I can pick up the words. *"Okay. Okay."*

"We have to get inside. I need you to help me."

He nods even though his eyes close. A second later, though, they're open again and he's trying to sit up.

I grab his forearm and stand, pulling him with me. It takes a lot of effort to get him on his feet, and once I do, he's unsteady. Weak. He should have stayed in bed. This infection has a stronger hold on him than we originally thought. Or maybe he's just worn out. Or the painkiller I gave him earlier has worn off. I don't know, but whatever it is, he needs to get back in bed and stay there. At least for a couple more days.

His body is so hot when he drapes his arm over my shoulder that my own body temperature shoots up at least ten degrees. The Tylenol must have worn off. Hopefully, that's all it is.

It's impossible to talk or encourage him to walk as we head toward the house, because I'm gritting my teeth. I'm bearing more of his weight than I should be able to—he has to weigh more than twice as much as me—and it's making my own legs unsteady.

It isn't far, though. I can do it. I've been through worse.

One thing I've learned over the last few months: telling yourself something doesn't make it true.

When we reach the porch I'm tempted to take a break, but I'm too afraid that if I put him down now, I won't be able to get him back up. So I keep moving, focusing on the door—thank God it's open—and dragging every ounce of energy I have inside me to the surface.

We make it inside and through the living room. Then we're in the kitchen, and Jim's body slumps against mine even more. I exhale, then suck a deep breath in and push him up. Keeping both of us from falling as we head toward the bedroom.

We barely make it through the door before Jim's legs give out and he tumbles forward, taking me with him. I hit the carpet, and he lands half on top of me. His body is completely slack, and even when I wiggle and grunt and shove my way out from under him, he doesn't move a muscle.

I'm gasping for air and panting by the time I sit up, but all I can think about is Jim. His face is pale and his mouth is hanging open. Fear rushes through me, nearly taking my breath away. Dear God, is he dead?

I lean down so my face is over his mouth and let out a sigh of relief when his warm breath caresses my cheek.

Please don't let him die. Please don't let him die.

I haven't begged God for help since the morning Michael died, but I'm not above doing it now. Even if He didn't listen to me last time around.

It takes a couple tries to roll Jim onto his back, but once I manage it, I feel better about leaving him. I have to get my rifle—which I foolishly dropped when I saw Jim collapse—and lock the front door. Then I need to get him some more medicine and quite possibly a dressing change.

"I'll be back, Jim," I say even though there's no way he can hear me, and then I take off running.

THE BED MOVES AND I JERK AWAKE, MY EYES FLYING open to meet the dark ceiling above me. Light from the candle on the bedside table flickers across the room, creating shadows that are terrifyingly long. Like goblins ready to jump out at me. It makes my heart beat harder.

At my side, Jim shifts again, and I twist his way to find him staring at me. Even in the limited light I can tell that his eyes are still hazy and feverish, but better than before. When his lips move, though, they're slow. Like he's slurring his words. The only part I catch is *saving my life*.

"Say it again."

Jim's Adam's apple bobs when he closes his eyes. When he opens them, he tries again. *"If you keep saving my life like this, I'm never going to be able to pay you back."*

"You saved my life today. From those men."

He shakes his head, and a drop of sweat rolls down the side of his face. *"No. I risked your life by letting my guard down."*

"That's debatable." Truth be told, we both let our guards down. I push myself up to a sitting position so I can feel his head. "How are you?" His skin is warm and clammy against my palm, but not on fire the way it was earlier.

Jim's lips move, but I have to turn his face toward me. He doesn't need me to tell him to repeat it. *"Like shit."*

That's what I was afraid of. He seemed to be doing better, but the infection may have gotten a second wind. Hopefully, the rest of the antibiotics I have do the trick. It's not like we have any other options, and even after one day of him being coherent, I've gotten shockingly used to having him around.

"You need to rest," I say. "No more getting up."

Jim smiles, but it's strained and painful. *"Yes, mom."*

He's a smart ass. I bet it got him in all kinds of trouble when he was a kid. Which actually reminds me of what we were talking about before those men showed up. Jim was giving me a hard time about the cigarette, but when I mentioned the trouble he must have gotten into as a kid, his mood changed. It was like a switch, and it makes me wonder about him. About where he's been and who he was before all this.

Not that right now is the time to get into it. He's burning up with fever, and if I want him to get better I'm going to have to make sure he finishes the meds Dad left behind. Some Tylenol for the fever would be good too. Make him feel better.

I move to get up, but Jim grabs my arm and I'm forced to turn toward him. His eyes are huge and clear. *"Where are you going?"*

"I want to get you another dose of antibiotics and some Tylenol." I point toward the bathroom, and Jim lets go.

"I thought you were leaving." His eyes drift shut.

He's out when I come back, and even though I know he needs his rest, I shake him awake. His eyes flutter open, focusing on me, and I hold out the pills. When he doesn't sit up right away, I help him. Three pills, two for the fever and his next dose of antibiotics, and then he can go back to sleep.

I hold the cup so he can wash the pills down, and his hand wraps around my wrist like he's holding on for dear life. The touch of his warm skin against mine is so nice after so many days of being alone that I don't want him to let go, but the second he's finished drinking, he does.

He plops back on the bed, his eyes closed before his head has even hit the pillow, and I stand over him. Holding the cup. Staring at him like I'm trying to unravel the puzzle of emotions and questions swirling through me. I don't know who this man is, but somehow he's managed to get under my skin after just a few days together. No. Not days. Minutes. Just that short time on the porch was enough to make me want to do everything imaginable to keep him alive.

CHAPTER ELEVEN

JIM

The next time I wake, my head is a hell of a lot clearer, and Amira is curled up next to me in bed. Out like a light.

How long have I been asleep?

It's dark in the room, but with the window covered the way it is, that doesn't mean anything. The memory of Amira and me sitting on the porch comes back to me, but that feels like days ago. I also remember apologizing for letting my guard down or something ridiculous like that. I'm not even sure how much of what I said she understood. Or what I said out loud for that matter. It's all a bit of a blur.

Whether it was days or hours ago, I don't know, but I do know that I'm better now. Remarkably so, actually. The wound on my leg throbs, but it doesn't feel like flames are licking at my skin the way it did before, and the fuzziness in my brain has lifted. Maybe the fever finally broke for good.

Hopefully.

My bladder screams in agony when I move. Since I can't remember the last time I took a piss, I shouldn't be surprised. Before I went out on the porch probably, but I'm not even sure how long ago that was.

Careful not to shake the bed too much, I ease my body off the mattress, my eyes on Amira the entire time. If I can get up without waking her I'll be in the clear. Thankfully, she can't hear any of the noises I will most definitely make once I'm in the bathroom.

I pee in the dark, but once that's done, I can't help noticing how itchy my beard has gotten. Like my hair, it's grimy to the touch. It hasn't been trimmed in more than a week, and at this point it's so full of dirt and only God knows what else that it makes me cringe. A trim would be a good idea. If I can find a razor or some scissors.

Amira already has candles lined up on the counter, so all I have to do is find the matches and light them. The shock of seeing myself in the mirror makes me take a step back. I'm skin and bones, almost as bad as I was at the beginning of the apocalypse. Before I found Hope Springs. Even though Amira cleaned me up when she first dragged me inside, I have streaks of dirt on my face and neck. On top of that, my hair is so filthy it looks dark brown instead of blond, and the beard on my face could have secured me a part on *Duck Dynasty*. Even in prison I didn't look this bad.

A shave isn't the only thing I need.

I search the drawers until I find a pair of scissors, some soap, and a washcloth. The trim doesn't take long, and by the time I'm done, the white marble counter is covered in filthy little hairs. I wipe them away, then plug the sink so I can fill it from the jug of water sitting on the counter. It's only a couple inches deep, but it's enough water to get the washcloth wet and scrub my face and what's left of my beard. That isn't good enough, though, not with how grimy I feel, so I pull my shirt over my head and toss it aside. By the time I'm done with the upper part of my body, the water is so brown it makes my stomach turn. Even though I hate the idea of wasting water, I pull the drain and let it run out before filling it with fresh water. It just feels so damn good to be clean.

I'm in the middle of trying to figure out how to wash my hair when Amira walks in behind me. Her eyes hold mine in the mirror, and she smiles, lighting up her face.

Damn she's pretty.

The thought catches me so off guard that I almost look away. I'm practically naked, but it's nothing she hasn't seen before and she doesn't seem to be shying away from it.

I turn to face her, waving toward the greasy mop on my head. "I wanted to wash my hair."

"I can help." She motions toward the tub. "Kneel there."

"I don't want to waste any more water."

"It's spring in Georgia. It will probably rain tomorrow. We'll just collect more to boil."

"Tomorrow?" I say doubtfully. I know I've been inside a lot, but so far it's been nothing but clear skies and sunshine.

"Tomorrow." She motions toward the tub again.

This time, I do as she says and kneel on the floor. A shower would be ideal, but right now I'll take anything. Even in prison I got daily showers, but now everything is filthy. I never knew it would bother me this much, but it does. Being grungy all the time takes more getting used to than a person realizes.

When I'm on my knees, I lean forward so the upper half of my body is hanging over the tub. Amira pours just enough water over my head to wet my hair, and it's so cold that I let out a low whistle. Which she can't hear. A second later she's running her hands through my hair, working shampoo that smells like coconut into the filthy strands. It feels so damn good that I let out a groan. Thank God she can't hear that, because it's so low and primal that it sounds sexual, and damn if what she's doing doesn't feel good. Having her hands moving over my scalp, slowly massaging my head as her body presses up against me from behind. It wakes up parts of me that are in desperate need of attention.

The cold water she pours over my head is more than necessary to rinse out the dirt and shampoo, but it does nothing to calm the fire raging in my blood. She runs her hands through my hair again and then pours a little more water over my head. This time, the water that slides across the bottom of the tub is clearer, and the third time she does it, there's barely even a tint of dirt or shampoo in it.

Amira pours the last little bit of water over my head and then runs her hands through my hair, twisting the strands around her fingers to wring them out. Then she grabs a towel and slides it down my head, leaning even closer to me. When her breasts press against my back, I swear I almost lose it. I groan again and clench my hands into fists. Silently begging her to back away while also wanting her to move closer.

It's been too damn long since I've had sex.

"Okay," she says and steps back.

If it wasn't for the fact that my shorts feel like they're two sizes smaller than when I kneeled down, I'd be thrilled. Right now, though, I'm afraid she's going to think I'm some kind of sex fiend. First when she was cleaning my cut, now this. Shit. It's like I'm fourteen all over again.

I work the towel through my hair as I get to my feet, tossing it aside when I've turned to face her completely. Her gaze is right where I thought it would be, and a pink flush creeps across her face that makes my blood boil even more. I don't think she's a teenager anymore—she's way too capable—but I can't help wishing I could still think of her that way. Maybe then I wouldn't be so damn turned on every time she got near me.

I step forward and gently grab her chin, tilting her face up so she's looking me in the eye. "Thank you."

"You're better?" she says, her gaze moving over my face. "No more fever?"

"No."

Amira nods and then takes a step back, her chin sliding out of my grasp. "I should get you something to eat."

I want to stop her from turning away from me. Want to

80

grab her and throw her down and do all kinds of dirty things to her. I'd love to make her scream my name while she begged for more.

But I don't.

CHAPTER TWELVE

AMIRA

This is something I never considered when I dragged Jim into my house. Sexual tension. Why would I? It's the apocalypse. We have bigger things to worry about. More important things to focus on than primal needs.

That doesn't mean those needs ceased to exist when most of the population died off. I just never thought about it before. Now that Jim's here and up and moving around, it seems to be constantly in the back of my mind. I can still feel the warmth that soaked into my body when I was pressed against him, washing his hair. The way his sigh echoed through me was enough to make me want to take my own clothes off. It was so deep and urgent.

I stare at the canned goods lining the shelves longer than necessary, almost unable to move. There are only a handful of cans left — I'm going through the stuff I found a lot faster now that Jim's here — but the food isn't what makes me hide in the closet. I need time to collect myself. To decide what, if anything, I'm going to do about this.

The way I see it, there are two options: address it or ignore it.

Talking to Jim about what's happening between us will be awkward, but worse than that, I also have serious doubts that it will get us anywhere. Plus, if we talk about it, from here on out we'll both be aware of the fact that the other person knows it's happening. Every second of every day, I will know that Jim knows I want him. Or that my body wants him, at least. Whether or not I actually like this man is another thing altogether. He has me intrigued and wanting to know more, but that's as far as we've gotten right now. Maybe as far as we'll ever get.

Ignoring it will be like existing with a shadow over us, but it would probably be better in the long run. This way, we can live in quiet ignorance, pretending that we're not checking the other person out every chance we get. Maybe, if we're lucky, it will pass and we'll never have to talk about it at all.

With my mind made up, I grab a can of chicken noodle soup off the shelf and head back into the bedroom. Thankfully, Jim is dressed.

When he looks up, he smiles. *"I found this in the dresser. I hope it's okay."*

He waves to the shirt, which I have a hard time focusing on because I'm still picturing the tattoos covering his arms and the way the muscles in his biceps flexed as he moved. He's lost weight from being sick, but the definition is still there. Not that it matters. Apparently I've reverted to the state of horny teenage girl, because I'm pretty sure I'd want him even if he didn't look like a character straight out of some romance novel featuring the hot bad boy next door.

"It's fine. Use anything you need," I say while thinking, *it's always okay for you to put clothes on.*

Jim pulls at the t-shirt, which is way too big for him, and all my thoughts about his hot body melt away as a pang shoots through me. It was Dad's shirt, and it looks big and awkward on the man in front of me. This man should be wearing leather, or at the very least all black. I can picture him in a well-worn, soft, black shirt that is so fitted it clings to the hard muscles of his arms and torso, showing off the tats snaking up his arms.

The shirt he put on, however, is bright white, and the fabric is stiff. It's also about three sizes too big. The words *Sammy's Bar-B-Q* are printed across the front, but I can't for the life of me remember us ever eating at a place by that name. Maybe Mom and Dad went there while I was away at school. Anything is possible.

Jim waves his hand in front of me, and my eyes snap up to his face. *"You okay?"*

My insides feel like someone dropped them into a blender, but I nod. "Yes," I say as I head for the kitchen. "Let's eat."

Even though I can't hear his footsteps, I can actually feel it when Jim follows me. It's like the heat from his body is able to reach out and caress me from four feet away, and it's comforting. Knowing someone else is in the house with me. That I don't have to look over my shoulder every two seconds.

Jim stands at my side in the kitchen while I dump the soup into the waiting pot. I add water, focusing on what I'm doing as I turn on the little camp stove. Ignoring how close to me he is. How my insides—that only moments ago felt raw and painful—are now buzzing with life just from having him next to me.

Once the stove is on, Jim touches my arm, and I'm forced to look into his soft, blue eyes. *"It's lucky that you have the stove. Where did you get it?"*

"My dad and mom liked to go camping, so we already had the stove. After the electricity went out, Dad went into town and stocked up on supplies. More propane, and some other survival gear."

Jim nods as I talk, and each time his eyes move from my face to sweep over my body, heat spreads through me. I look down, trying to figure out what he might be thinking, but I just look like me. Shorts that are comfy and a little big—nice for lounging in—and a t-shirt that has seen better days but is soft. As far as I'm concerned, there's nothing about me that should really attract this man. I'm not foolish enough to think I'm not attractive, but I'm not interesting. I don't have scars and tattoos that tell stories about the life I lived before all this, and if I were being honest, I'd admit that I never really had much of a life. Especially not now.

When I meet Jim's eyes again, he tilts his head to the side like he too is trying to figure me out. *"What are you thinking?"*

The expression on his face tells me he knows exactly what I'm thinking. Is he asking because he wants me to give him the okay?

"Nothing." My body is boiling when I turn back to find steam rising off the soup.

When I pull the pot off the stove, my hands are shaking so badly that I'm afraid I'm going to drop it and scald us both. Luckily, I manage to get it on the counter without any major injury. I turn the stove off while Jim divides the soup between two bowls, focusing on what I'm doing so I don't have to look at him. Hoping the desire swirling through me will fade if I pretend it doesn't exist.

We sit at the table with our bowls, something I haven't done since the early days of the virus. It makes me uneasy, being so close to the sliding glass door, knowing someone could peek in through the windows and see the two of us sitting here. But it isn't just that. It's the feeling that we're playing a game. House or dress-up or tea party, or something else just as childish. Only it isn't child's play, because I know what we both want the outcome of this game to be.

I sip the soup off my spoon, focusing on the living room and the basket of Legos I still haven't spread back out. Avoiding looking at the man across from me. The whole time, my mind is spinning like a wheel. Flipping through

86

everything I've done since the virus broke out, everything Dad and I set up, and all the scenarios we planned for. This was never one of them. Dad disappearing and another man popping up. Now that it's happened, I'm not quite sure what to do.

Jim touches my arm, and it startles me so much that I jerk away, spilling hot soup all over my arm. Heat somehow spreads from my arms to my neck, then up over my cheeks as I wipe the liquid up. Still avoiding looking directly at Jim.

But I can't avoid looking at him forever, and once I've cleaned myself up, I turn to find his striking blue eyes on me. *"Sorry, I didn't mean to scare you. I just wanted to know what's going on. You seem uneasy."*

I shrug like I'm not sure where my mind was even though I do know. "My dad, mostly. I'm not sure how he would react if he knew I brought you into the house."

Jim's eyebrows shoot up, and once again a flush spreads across my face. I hadn't thought the words through before I said them, but now that I turn them over in my head, I realize what they could imply. That Dad would think this was inappropriate because Jim is a man and I'm a woman, and we're alone. That something could happen. It's the exact subject that I wanted to avoid.

Jim runs his hand through his mostly dry hair, and I notice for the first time that I was right. It is lighter than it looked before. Dark blond and thick. My fingers twitch with the desire to feel the soft strands, but I busy them by picking my spoon back up and taking another sip.

Jim touches my arm again, and even though it doesn't startle me this time, it does send a jolt of electricity shooting through my body.

"Once I have a little more energy back, we can head out."

Head out? I shake my head, and when Jim repeats it, I realize he thinks I didn't understand him. Which is true, but not because I didn't catch the words. Because it never occurred to me that he'd want to leave this house. I've been good here, and heading out into the unknown world doesn't seem like a good idea. Especially when I think about the condition Jim was in when I found him.

"Where do you want to go?"

Jim has the same reaction I did just a second ago: he shakes his head. I guess we're not on the same page at all.

"*To Atlanta.*" He puts his hand over mine, and my skin sizzles under his touch. "*I thought I told you where I was headed, but maybe that was a dream. The CDC is still working, and they have a wall around the city. They're trying to start over.*"

A wall around the city...

That he hadn't told me, but I'm not sure it makes a whole lot of sense. We're 300 miles from Atlanta, and every inch of road between here and there is infested with zombies. Dad went out, and he never came back.

No. I promised my father that if he didn't make it, I'd do everything in my power to make sure I got out of this alive. And I meant it. I can't risk my life by going out there.

"I'm safe here. I have everything I need."

Jim's fingers wrap around mine until my digits are almost crushed under his grip. "*You're safe for now, but what happens when someone finds you? Those men came. There could be more. Plus, you can't live your entire life in the attic.*"

"No one found me until I brought you here." I lift my chin as I pry my hand from his. "Those men were the first people I've seen in weeks. And the zombies have been almost as rare. Just a handful."

I swallow when the image of the man I killed comes screaming back. He was shot, thanks to Jim, but he tried to get up, and the gleam in his eye was murderous. I slit his throat and I'd do it again, but I can't stop my body from trembling when I think about how I took a man's life. This isn't how the world is supposed to be. I'm not supposed to have to kill to protect my house.

Jim touches my arm again, and I look up, realizing my gaze has drifted away. "*There are people out there. People who will do horrible things to you.*" He shakes his head so hard that a chunk of hair falls into his eyes, and when he brushes it away, it's almost violent. *"The people I was with before ran into a really nasty group in Vegas. I don't know the whole story, but I know they barely made it out alive. And I also know that can't be the only group out there like that. People are bad. Trust me."*

Nothing he's saying surprises me, which is part of the reason I don't want to leave. Here, I'm securely tucked away in a corner of the world that few people have discovered. Out there, people will prey on you.

"If I stay here, people like that won't be able to find me."

I get up so he knows the conversation is over and take my bowl into the kitchen.

Only a second after putting my bowl down, Jim is at my side, but I stare out the window. His hand brushes my arm, and it's so gentle that goose bumps pop up on my skin. Still, I keep my eyes straight ahead. Through the window the backyard is visible, and the field beyond that. Little white and yellow flowers break up the monotony of the green grass and weeds, and as the wind sweeps over the landscape, they all bow to its will. It's mesmerizing, watching the breeze blow across the field.

Jim forces me to turn and grabs my chin in his hand. When my eyes are locked with his, he steps closer, pinning me against the counter with his body. The heat between us is so intense it makes my knees wobble.

"I won't leave you here to die." He lets out a deep breath. *"But I think staying is a bad idea. Think about it. Okay?"*

For me, there's nothing to think about, but his gaze is so penetrating that I find myself nodding. He shifts and his hand falls away, but he doesn't tear his gaze from mine, and his body is still pressed against me. When his eyes finally move, it's only so they can travel over my lips. The idea of lifting myself up on the tips of my toes and kissing him is so tempting that I have a hard time controlling myself, but I do. Somehow.

"We're going to need food soon," I say, breaking the spell by gently pushing him away from me.

Jim takes a step back. *"Is there a town nearby?"*

"Yes. About three miles from here. I rode my bike there the day I found you."

"*Bike?*" Jim shakes his head like I'm crazy. "*That's too dangerous.*"

"For me, driving would be too dangerous. I don't understand sounds the way you do. Remember?"

"*I never thought about it like that.*" He lets out a deep breath, and when his eyes cloud over, I'm shocked by how much concern there is. Is he worried about me? "*This is a dangerous world for you. I wish you'd understand that leaving is the best option.*"

"For you. Not for me."

"*Whatever. You promised to think about it.*" Jim glances over his shoulder, and when he looks back he says, "*Is there gas in that SUV?*"

"My dad filled up both cars before the gas was all gone. He knew we might need it."

"*Both?*"

"The other one disappeared when he did."

Jim frowns, and I can tell he's hesitant to ask any questions, but that doesn't stop him. '*What happened to him? To your dad?*"

"I told you. He left to get supplies." I let out a deep breath when grief tries to claw its way to the surface, hoping to blow it out or stifle it or something. Anything to keep the tears away. "We were low on water, so he left me here. That's all I know. When he didn't come back that night, I thought he had just gotten hung up. It had happened before." I cringe, remembering the first time he got delayed, but shake it off so I can continue with my story. "But he didn't come back the next day, or the next, and now it's been over a week. Still, it hasn't been that long. He could come back." I look away when doubt flashes in Jim's eyes. He thinks I'm fooling myself. Maybe I am. "It's why I can't leave."

Jim grabs my arm and I turn back to face him even though I don't want to know what he's thinking. "*What did you do for food? You said you were almost out when your dad left,*" *but you have plenty now."*

I almost laugh, so relieved he isn't calling me out for being delusional.

"I put off going out as long as I could, but eventually I had to do it. The town is over four miles away and I was scared out of my mind, but my dad worked hard to teach me what makes noise and what doesn't. The last time I went out with him, zombies almost overran me, but it taught me an important lesson. Never rush. I have little tricks that keep me safe now, and I stick to them. Religiously."

Jim's eyes move down as he nods, and I follow his gaze to the flour spread across the floor. His footprints are still there from the day he went out on the porch, and the once carefully spread-out white powder is scattered as far as the living room. There's also a nice trail that leads to the master bedroom.

"I put it there," I say before he can ask. "I spread the flour all over the floor so I'd know if someone had walked through the house. And I did the same thing upstairs, only with dirt from a plant."

When I look up, he's smiling at me. *"You're a genius."*

I laugh and roll my eyes and shake my head all at the same time so he'll know exactly how ridiculous I think that statement is. "No, I just figured out how to adapt to my environment. I've always had to do it, and an apocalypse is no different."

The smirk Jim gives me says he doesn't buy it. He can think what he wants, but I know I'm no genius. I just want to live.

Jim touches my arm, his fingers barely grazing my elbow. It's so soft and gentle that it sends warmth shooting through me. Unlike earlier, though, this isn't sexual. It's just the comfort of knowing that I'm not alone anymore.

"We'll take the car and drive to this town. We can load up on supplies that way. Okay?"

"Now?" It's afternoon, but we have plenty of daylight

left. Driving will also mean it shouldn't take nearly as much time as it took me the other day.

Jim frowns. *"Do you want to wait?"*

"No. Now's as good a time as any."

CHAPTER THIRTEEN

JIM

At least now I know why Amira is so reluctant to leave. She's still hoping her dad will come back. It's a fool's dream, but I'm not going to run out on her. Maybe she doesn't believe there's any real danger here, but I know there is. Nowhere is safe anymore, and if Jon and his group taught me anything, it's that we have to band together if we want to survive.

I chuckle to myself. Before all this, I sure as hell never thought I'd see things that way. I was never exactly the play-by-the-rules or work-well-with-others kind of guy. Crazy how the apocalypse can change things like that.

Amira gives me a questioning look, but I shake my head as I lay the bullets out on the table in front of me. There aren't a lot left, and I'd love to get something a little more powerful than this .22.

"This is the only gun you have?" I ask, careful to talk slow and keep my face toward her so she can catch every word.

She nods, and I swear under my breath, fully aware that the tone of my voice doesn't matter and she'll still be able to read the curse coming out of my mouth.

"What's wrong?" she asks, frowning.

It causes her eyebrows to pull down, and a shadow spreads across her forehead and almost gives off the impression that she has a unibrow. Not that it makes me any less attracted to her. At this point, there isn't a lot that could, and it only partly has to do with the fact that I haven't had sex in a long fucking time.

I shake my head and force my brain to focus on thoughts that don't revolve around the two of us naked. It's probably one of the most difficult things I've ever had to do.

"A twenty-two doesn't pack much of a punch, but it's better than nothing. Maybe we'll get lucky and find something else." Not that I'm holding my breath. Things are pretty picked over at this point.

Amira frowns again as she twists her hair around her hand and pulls it back into a ponytail. I do my best not to stare when her shirt rides up, revealing the soft, brown skin of her stomach. Trying not to think about how her body felt when it was pressed up against mine just a few minutes ago in the kitchen.

"My dad had a friend who lived about five miles from here," she says, pulling my thoughts to the present. "He liked guns. Maybe we could check his place out?"

"Is it on our way to town or in the other direction?"

"The other direction. But he could have food too." She shrugs. "It's worth a try, right?"

It is, and finding something other than this .22 could be a lifesaver. I get why Amira's dad picked the thing up. It doesn't have the kickback that a bigger caliber gun would have, so it's probably a lot easier for a girl who's out here on her own. Which her dad must have known was a possibility when he went out and left her here all by herself.

94

"Okay, then." I throw the rifle over my shoulder. "We'll head that way first."

Amira nods and starts to follow me when I head for the garage, but stops after a couple steps. When I turn, I find her looking around. Studying the house like she isn't sure she wants to leave it.

I tap her on the shoulder, and when she's facing me, say, "What's wrong?"

"I don't know. I just feel like I'm saying goodbye for good. Is that weird?"

I press my lips together before what I'm thinking forces its way out. It's not weird because every time you leave a place, it could be the last time you see it.

"We'll be back in a few hours," I say instead, giving her shoulder a squeeze. "Don't worry."

Amira nods, and this time when I head for the garage, she's right behind me. She stops just before stepping through the door and grabs a book bag off a hook. Her name is above it, and mounted on the wall right next to hers hangs a second hook, this one empty. The name above it is Michael.

I point to the hook when Amira turns to face me. "Your brother?"

Her eyes dart away as she nods. I get the feeling that she doesn't want to share that part of her life me, and for some reason it stings. Like the fact that she's holding a part of herself back is a betrayal. Which is dumb. There's a whole airplane full of baggage I haven't shared with her, and I'm not planning to, either.

Amira climbs into the passenger seat while I head over to the garage door. Since the chain has already been detached from the opener, all I have to do is pull the thing open. It's heavy, and the weight of it sends a sharp pain shooting up and down my leg. The damn door is halfway up before it hits me that I should have checked to make sure the coast was clear first.

That's a mistake that shouldn't ever be made.

The second the door is up, I grab the rifle off my back and swing it around just in case. Outside, the yard is clear of everything but nature. Thankfully. I need to be smarter than this from here on out.

Slipping behind the wheel of the car is an odd feeling. It's been probably six months since I drove, before I got to Hope Springs, and even then it was only a few times. Before that, I was sitting in a jail cell rotting away.

"Hope I still know how to do this," I mutter as I slip the key into the ignition.

Amira touches my arm, and when I turn to look at her, she shakes her head, her eyes on my lips as usual. Something about the closeness of the car and the intensity of her gaze makes me squirm as images of the two of us are flung at me from all directions, each one of them dirtier than the last.

Not good. I have to stop thinking about her like that.

"Just talking to myself," I say. "Nothing important."

She frowns, but nods to let me know she understands.

She probably doesn't, though. I can't imagine deaf people walking around talking to themselves. I'm pretty sure I do it just to feel like I'm not alone in this world, which means there's no point if you can't hear the sound of your own voice.

I turn the key and the engine roars to life. Amira was right when she said her dad had filled up the tank. The needle is just under the F on the gas gauge. Lucky for us. If I can get her to agree to go to Atlanta, we should be able to drive the whole way there.

I pull out and put the SUV into park, then run back and pull the garage door shut. The whole process takes less than a minute, and once I'm back inside, I throw the car into drive.

Amira points left and I do what I'm told, turning onto the main road and heading off. With no other cars and no cops to worry about, I could drive as fast as I wanted, but I stay close to sixty so I don't miss any turns. It's not like I know where I'm going.

"Left up here," she says after we've driven a couple minutes in silence.

It's odd how fast I've gotten used to being with her and not talking all the time. It's something most people don't know how to do, especially now when every conversation might be your last. Every time we went out to clear the streets in Hope Springs, Jon would do his best to try and get me to spill my guts about anything and everything.

I slow and take a left, and Amira scoots to the edge of her seat. She peers out the window like she's looking for something, so I keep my speed closer to forty while I wait for instructions.

After about a minute, she points out the window. "Next one. On the right."

I turn into the driveway, passing a mailbox that says *The Millers* and slowing to a stop so we can get a feel for the place. The sun is bright and right behind the house, making it tough to get a good look at it, but from what I can tell, nothing's moving.

"What now?" Amira asks.

I turn her way, and her gaze zooms in on my lips. "We'll go in nice and slow. Stick close to me. Got it?"

When she nods, I put the car in gear.

Going anywhere unknown makes me uneasy, but not knowing exactly how the person I'm with operates is even worse. When I was with Jon, we had a system, but Amira is an unknown that I hadn't planned on or expected.

In more ways than one.

I park in front of the house and turn the car off, but neither one of us moves, and the fact that she doesn't throw the door open and run out makes me feel better about the whole thing. She said she was careful, and I'm glad to discover she wasn't just talking out of her ass.

Nothing moves either around us or inside. The house is huge. One of those places that makes you wonder what the owners did to make their money and why they hell they chose to live out in the middle of nowhere. I'm hoping the reason for this guy's seclusion is directly related to his love of guns. If so, it could mean we hit the mother load.

I touch Amira's knee to get her attention, and she tears her gaze from the house so she can look at my lips. "Ready?"

She nods once before turning to the door, and then we're both climbing out. I have the rifle and a pocket full of extra bullets, but it doesn't make me feel very secure. I can only get one good shot off before I have to reload. Not great odds if we bump into a horde.

We head for the house, walking side by side, and every sound has my heart pounding faster. A rock clinks across the driveway when Amira accidently kicks it, hitting the aluminum siding on the house with a ping that echoes across the open field. Tree branches scrape against the roof, and the twinkling of an unseen wind chime joins every breeze that sweeps across the yard.

We stop on the porch and look in through the picture window. On the other side of the glass sits a dining room table that is covered in a thick layer of dust, and just past that, the kitchen is visible through the doorway. It's dark inside, and still. Probably empty, but there's only one way to know for sure.

I rap my knuckles against the glass and Amira gives me a sharp look, but I'm too focused on the inside of the house to ask her what it's for. When nothing moves I head for the front door, but the knocking of Amira's knuckles against the window makes me turn.

She doesn't look my way—she's too focused on the window—but she does hold one finger up. I wait, keeping an eye on the yard while she searches for whatever she's looking for. After a couple seconds, she heads for the front door.

When she turns the knob, I tense, but the thing doesn't budge. We step back at the exact same time and look the house over.

"Break the window." Amira's voice is so loud that I nearly shit myself, and it echoes through the still day, moving out across the fields and calling out to every damn zom within a mile.

No wonder her dad told her to use sign language.

"Yeah," I say, swallowing the lump that has managed to lodge itself in my throat.

It doesn't make a whole lot of sense to waste time looking for an easy way in. We could spend fifteen minutes trying to find a way inside only to end up having to break the damn window anyway. Might as well just go for it.

I spot a large decorative rock in the garden lining the porch and hand the rifle to Amira. It takes a couple seconds to pry the thing out of the dirt, but once I do, I carry it over to the window and heave it toward the glass. The crack that echoes through the air when the rock goes flying into the dining room is so loud it almost makes me jump. Shards rain down, scattering across the ground in front of us and the dining room floor.

I turn toward Amira and wave at the glass spread across the porch. "Careful."

The glass crunches under my boots when I climb through the window, being careful to avoid the shards still stuck in the frame. The second I'm through, Amira passes me the rifle and climbs in behind me, ducking under the glass hanging down from above. A shard at the bottom comes within an inch of slicing her leg open, but somehow she manages to make it inside in one piece.

Once in, Amira steps in front of me. "This way."

Again, her voice carries much farther than it should. My heart rate, which has already reached dangerous proportions, goes up about ten more notches. I follow her quietly though, knowing that trying to explain how loud her voice is in the empty house would be useless.

Learning some of that sign language is sounding like a better idea by the second.

She leads me from the dining room to a big living room then into the kitchen, where she stops in front of a closed door. She reaches for the knob, but I grab her arm before she can turn it.

"Wait," I whisper when she looks my way. "And try not

to talk anymore. Let's use hand signals as much as possible."

Amira nods and points toward the door.

"I know. Just open it nice and easy."

She nods again and turns the knob, watching me for a signal that it's okay to pull the door open. I step back and aim the rifle at the opening just in case. When I'm ready, I give her a nod, and Amira eases the door open. My body tenses and my finger moves to the trigger, but when nothing comes charging out at me, I relax.

Amira pulls out a flashlight and aims it at the dark opening. In front of us, stairs descend into the blackness of a basement.

Even though I keep my eyes on the dark stairs in front of us, I make sure I turn my face toward her when I say, "I'll go first."

She steps back to give me space, aiming the flashlight on the stairs, and I head down, keeping my rifle up and ready. Behind me, Amira holds the flashlight steady, lighting the way. The steps are carpeted, masking the sound of our steps, and they lead into a finished basement that's set up like a home theater. Two rows of leather recliners face a screen mounted on the wall that is bigger than my jail cell was.

I barely have time to process it though, because within seconds of setting foot in the basement, Amira grabs my arm. She jerks me around, and the beam of her flashlight bobs across the room. She doesn't let go of me until she has me turned all the way around, facing the opposite direction. Even then she won't stop panning the flashlight around. It's moving so fast it's making me dizzy, but it's pitch black, so I can't ask her what's wrong. I just know something is.

"Zombie."

The strangled word cuts through the darkness, and my finger moves back to the trigger. I don't see anything, and the basement is as silent as the upstairs was.

"Where the hell is it?" My words echo through the basement, nearly scaring the shit out of me, but I still don't see or hear a thing. What the hell has her so freaked out?

My heart is pounding so fast that it feels like it's going to explode. I let out a deep breath, hoping to calm myself, and when I suck air back in through my nose, I smell it. Rot. It's faint, but it's there. *That's* what has Amira so worried.

Hoping she'll be able to see me, I wave to the far corner of the room where I saw a door. When she doesn't stop moving the flashlight around, I grab hold of her arm and force her to point the beam at the door. When I let go, she keeps the flashlight focused on the door, but the beam still bobs up and down like she's shaking. I can't blame her. She's depending on her sense of smell, which tells her there's trouble. But I can hear, so I know there's no movement down here. Whatever is stinking this place up isn't moving around.

I wave toward the door as I walk forward, and Amira slinks after me, her shoes scraping across the floor at my back like she's dragging her feet. I don't think there's anything to be worried about, but I take my time and listen. Even when we get closer, there's nothing but silence.

"Here we go," I say when I stop in front of the door.

CHAPTER FOURTEEN
AMIRA

It's times like this that I feel cut off from the world. Surrounded by nothingness. Locked in a world of silence.

The black basement has stolen one of the senses I depend on to survive, which is my ability to see, and as the darkness begins to close in on me, the panic starts to build. It gets even worse when Jim stops in front of the door. The stench may be faint, but it's there, and it has every inch of my body buzzing with the urge to flee.

Jim reaches for the doorknob, and I have to press my feet against the floor to keep them from moving. My hand, which was shaking before, is suddenly trembling so hard that the light starts bobbing up and down at a speed that reminds me of a hummingbird's wings. Jim stops with his hand still on the knob and glances my way. It's too dark to interpret the look, and his lips are cloaked in shadows. If he said something, I don't have a clue what it was.

"I'm okay," I say even though I'm not.

I'm not okay standing in a dark room where I'm cut off from everything, and I'm not okay waiting for Jim to open this door, not knowing if something is going to charge out and try to get us or if it's nothing more than a corpse.

Jim faces the door once again, and I suck in a deep breath. I let it out when he turns the knob and force my arm to stop moving. He shoves the door open, and the smell intensifies. I wait for the moment of terror that always hits when one of them comes charging, but nothing happens.

With the rifle pointed toward the dark room, Jim takes a step forward. He motions for me to follow and I do, keeping close but trying not to crowd him. If there is something in the room, he might need the space to wrestle it to the ground.

Every step we take forward makes my nose tingle from the stench and my stomach twist until it threatens to expel the soup I ate just an hour earlier. Back when I was in the safety of my own home. We step inside and I move the flashlight around, trying to find the source of the stink. Nothing moves, though. Not even in the corners.

Jim grabs my hand and points the beam across the room again, this time moving it slower. When he does, I'm able to get a better idea of where we are. A storage room of some sort. Shelves line the walls. Some have boxes on them that are labeled with things like *Christmas* and *Skiing*, while other shelves are crammed full of canned goods. Just seeing the rows and rows of food makes my stomach rumble so hard it vibrates through my body.

Halfway across the room, Jim stops moving my arm. The beam illuminates a rack of guns hanging on the wall. Under it, on another rack, are even more guns, as well as stacks of ammunition.

I see his lips move out of the corner of my eye, but I don't turn so I can find out what he said. The stench of death is still hanging in the room, and before we do anything else, I want to know what we're dealing with.

Pulling my hand from Jim's grasp, I pan the flashlight to

the left, sweeping it across the room. It isn't until I get to the last corner that I find what I've been looking for. A body, long dead and so decayed it's impossible to tell who it was, is slumped against the wall. A pistol is in its hand and a splash of blood—and probably brain matter—is spread across the wall behind it.

I elbow Jim and nod toward the body. "There."

His head bobs, and I think his lips move, but it's impossible to know what he's saying or if he's even talking to me. When he heads for the body, I stay where I am and work to keep my arm steady. It's decomposed and its brains were long ago splattered all over the wall, but that doesn't stop me from trembling as I watch Jim walk across the room.

He kneels in front of it, casting a shadow across both the body and the wall and blocking everything from my sight. I step to the left and try to give him more light, but his broad frame doesn't leave me much to work with from this far away. I'd have to step closer if I wanted to really help him out, which is something I don't want to do.

After a few seconds he stands, and when he turns around he's holding a pistol in one hand and a clip in the other. When he's done checking it for ammo, he slips the clip back into place and tucks the gun in the waistband of his pants. Then he heads toward the wall of weapons.

I follow, keeping the flashlight steady so he can see what he's doing. A lantern would be nice right about now.

Jim turns to face me, pulling the flashlight up so his face is illuminated. It casts dark shadows across his cheeks and makes his eyes appear sunken and empty. When his lips move, I'm standing so close to him and the shadows are so deep that it's impossible for me to figure out what he's saying.

"It's too dark," I say, taking a step back. Trying to shift the light so I can get a better look at him. In the small space and with just the flashlight, it's impossible, though. There are too many shadows, and I end up either blinding him or myself. "I'll just ask you a yes or no question. Okay?"

Jim nods.

105

"Are we going to take all the guns?"

He nods again.

"And the food?"

His head bobs for a third time.

"So we'll just start dragging it upstairs?"

This time, he smiles when he nods. His mouth moves, but he's already turning toward the wall of weapons, so I'm sure he's just talking to himself.

I prop the flashlight up on a shelf and search the room for something to put the food in but come up empty. Instead of heading into another part of the house to look around, I drag a box off the shelf and dump it on the floor. Strands of Christmas lights tumble out, along with a tree skirt and some garlands.

When I turn back around, Jim is grinning at me, but I don't know why and in the darkness of the basement it would be a waste of time to ask, so I just get busy loading the cans into the box while he starts dragging guns off the shelf.

By the time the box is full, it's too heavy for me to carry. Before I've even had a chance to ask Jim for help, he's at my side and holding a bag out to me. When I take it from him, I peer inside to find boxes of ammo and several handguns.

Jim hauls the box of food off the floor, and even in the darkness of the basement I can read his lips when he says, "*Shit.*"

I laugh. "Sorry. I know it's heavy."

He shrugs, then nods to the flashlight. I sweep it off the counter and turn the beam toward the doorway, lighting our way as we head out of the basement. Once we're on the first floor, I can breathe a little easier. And not just because of the smell. Being in such a dark space makes me feel confined. Trapped, even.

Jim and I load the food and guns into the back of the SUV, but before we turn to go inside, he grabs my elbow. "*Good work on finding this place.*"

"I can't believe I didn't think of it sooner, and I'm kind of shocked my dad never came here." I glance toward the house and frown. Maybe there was a reason Dad never raided this guy's basement.

Jim grabs my arm and turns me toward him. *What's wrong?*

"Nothing." I shake my head like I'm trying to jiggle the worry free. "You liked the gun selection?"

A grin spreads across Jim's face. *"Couldn't have picked them better myself. This guy loved guns. An Ak-47, AR-15, a couple glocks. Even an M1 carbine rifle, which will be a great replacement for the rifle you've been using. Shit."*

Is it weird that he can identify so many guns in the darkness of a basement?

"How do you know so much about guns?" I ask before I can think better of it.

The smile melts from Jim's face faster than a stick of butter in a hot skillet. *"No reason."*

It's a bold-faced lie, and one hard to ignore, but since we're in the middle of unloading more supplies than I'd dreamed of finding, I let it go. For now. Eventually, he's going to have to tell me something about himself, though.

"Let's finish up." I turn my back on him and head toward the house.

Jim walks so close to me as we head inside again that I can literally feel him. His heat. His scent. His masculinity seeps into me and fills my body with tingles that are hard to ignore.

When we descend into the basement, the stench of death is like a bucket of ice water being thrown on my face. I load up the rest of the food—courtesy of another emptied box—while Jim drags an armful of guns up to the car. I don't even know how many we're going to end up with, but if we wanted to start an army, I think we could.

Just as I put the last can in a cardboard box, a shadow falls over me. I turn, ready to tell Jim I'm done, only to find a hulk of a man standing above me, the beam of my flashlight directed right at his face, which is smeared in filth. His eyes, bloodshot and sunken, flash down at me, and the anger that radiates off him is so volatile that it feels like a punch in the gut.

Spittle flies from his mouth when his lips move, but the shadows are too pronounced for me to make out the words. I crawl back, hoping to put some distance between us, and bump into the shelves. My heart pounds until it feels like a hammer banging on the inside of my chest. I don't know who this man is, but it isn't Mr. Miller.

"Who are you?" I ask even though I know I won't be able to catch his response.

His mouth moves as he steps closer. I can't make out the words, but the tone is so clear I couldn't miss it. His body shakes when he talks and his hands clench into fists so tight he looks like he's ready to step into a boxing ring. He reaches down and wraps his hand around my bicep, jerking me to my feet. Pain shoots through my arm, and I scream Jim's name so loudly that it practically makes my teeth vibrate.

The man slams my back against the shelf, yelling in my face. His breath is as foul as the body rotting on the other side of the room, and every time he talks, spit sprays across my cheeks. His fingers sink into my arms as he leans closer, getting less than an inch from me. The heat from his breath slams into me, and I turn my face away. Squeeze my eyes shut. Clench my hands into fists. Hold my breath. Try to block everything out.

This is it. Jim is obviously dead or he would have come running by now, which means I've reached my end.

I should have stayed in the house.

Suddenly, so fast that I barely register what's happening, the man is ripped away from me. I hit the ground just as my eyes fly open. Two figures struggle in the shadows of the room, just beyond the reach of the flashlight. As I watch, one slams the other into the ground and rams a fist into his face. Over and over again, so many times that the movement radiates all the way across the room to where I'm sitting. I press my back into the shelf, which shudders under the pressure.

108

Is it Jim?

If it is, none of this makes sense. Where the hell did this guy come from, and why didn't he kill Jim when he found him upstairs?

After a few seconds, the man on the floor stops moving, and the one standing over him steps away. He's still in the shadows, but I've come to know the outline of my companion so well at this point that the second he steps closer to the light, I'm able to discern Jim's shape. His hands are still clenched at his sides and his shoulders heave with every breath he lets out, but it's him.

"Jim!"

He turns away from the man on the floor and drops to his knees in front of me, directly into the beam of my flashlight. His blue eyes move over me, checking me from head to toe before stopping on my face.

"*You okay?*" His words are so clear that I can almost imagine I heard them.

"Yes." I swallow when I look past him to the man. He isn't moving. "Is he dead?"

Jim shakes his head as he gets to his feet, pulling me with him. He starts to move toward me, and for a second I think he's going to pull me in for a hug, but instead he grabs the box of food off the floor. When he's standing again, he nods toward the door.

I swipe up the flashlight and hurry after him, anxious to be out of the dark basement so we can talk again.

Jim moves so fast that it's hard for me to keep up, and he doesn't slow even when we've reached the first floor. When we make it outside, I finally run in front of him, blocking his way so he has to talk to me.

"Stop," I say. "What was that?"

Jim shakes his head, his eyes focused on the box of food in his hands. "*I don't know, but he was raving like a lunatic. Yelling things that didn't make sense. I think he was out of his mind. I'm not even sure where he came from.*"

"Where were you?"

He closes his eyes for a second and swallows. *"Upstairs. I just wanted to check things out before we left. I thought you'd be safe for a few minutes. I'm sorry."*

He left me alone in the basement? In the darkness where I couldn't see or hear? The pain that shoots through me is sharper than the prick of a needle.

"I can't hear."

Jim's eyes fly open. *"You don't have to remind me of that."*

"Obviously I do!" My hands move on their own. I don't even think about it as I sign the words coming out of my mouth. "You dragged me out here. You told me you would be my ears. You told me I was safer with you than in my attic. Then you left me alone."

His jaw clenches, and his eyes move past me to the car. Even though I don't want to let him off so easily, I turn. A few figures are visible in the distance, so far away that it should be impossible to know what they are, but it's not. Their slow gait gives them away.

When I look back at Jim he says, *"We should go."*

Of course. God forbid the conversation ever gets turned around on him.

I spin on my heel and head for the car, leaving him standing where he is. He's just reached the back of the SUV when I climb into the passenger seat, and the whole thing shifts when the back door slams.

CHAPTER FIFTEEN

JIM

The trembling that started in my body the second I heard Amira scream hasn't faded. It's so violent that it overshadows the weariness in my limbs and the ache radiating from the still-healing cut on my thigh.

I pause behind the SUV and pull out a cigarette, lighting it as I watch the zombies in the distance. They move closer, inch by inch. Even from this far away, their moans are carried on the wind. Moans Amira can't hear.

I inhale deeply, sucking the smoke into my lungs as I turn my back on the zoms. Shit. I'm an even bigger asshole than I thought I was.

This is a new thing for me, the feeling that I almost lost something big, and I don't quite know what to make of it. The attraction I feel toward her is natural. Human. But the ache that refuses to ease when I think about what could have happened is different. It's like a piece of myself was almost torn away.

I toss the still-smoking cigarette on the ground before climbing into the driver's seat. When I glance Amira's way, she's staring out the passenger window. Her arms are crossed, and between that and the tears shimmering on her cheeks, she's back to looking like a scared child. I haven't seen her in that light in a while. She's been too capable and strong and resilient lately for me to think of her as anything other than a woman. She wasn't someone who needed protection to me. But now, listening to her sniffles, all I want to do is keep her safe.

Even though every inch of me wants to force her to turn my way so I can tell her I'm sorry and beg for her forgiveness, I don't. I just start the SUV and do a U-turn, heading back up the driveway so we can get home. Back to safety. Or what she thinks of as safety, anyway.

The silence that accompanies us on the drive back is different than the one from the way here. Now, every time she shifts in her seat or exhales, I have to grit my teeth to keep from cursing. Both at myself and at the stupidity of this whole situation. It's ridiculous. Me wanting to protect a woman I barely know and her being pissed that I'm not the knight in shining armor she thought I would be. I could have told her before we left the house that I would never be able to play that role.

We make it back and find the yard once again empty. The silence continues after I get the garage door open and pull the SUV in, hanging over us as we get busy unloading. The longer it stretches out, the more I want to scream.

The second we've brought the last box into the house though, Amira is on me. "I've let it go long enough, but after today I have to know who you are."

"What the hell is that supposed to mean?" I ask, trying to back away but getting nowhere. Even with the whole living room behind me, I feel cornered.

"You know what I mean. Every time I ask you about your

past, you dodge the question or change the subject. You have scars that healed long before the zombies showed up, and you know more about guns than the average person. You have a dark past, and I want to know what it is."

The way she stares at my lips makes me uneasy in a way I don't understand. Ready to bolt, but ready to die for her at the same time. Wanting to throw her on the ground. I'm not sure. I just know I need her to look at me like that either forever or never again.

I look away from her intense brown eyes, focusing on the wall above her so I don't have to think about what's going on between us and how much potential it has to hurt us both.

"Why does it matter who I was?" I shove my hand through my hair and keep my face turned toward her so she can catch my words.

"Because you want me to leave this house and go to Atlanta with you," she says. "Because you want me to trust you, but I don't know who you are and it's obvious you don't trust me."

"It's not about trust," I say, keeping my eyes on the wall. "It's because that person doesn't exist anymore. It's all in the past, and I want it to stay that way."

Amira grabs my chin and jerks my face down, and I'm forced to finally meet her eyes, which are dark and full of light and hope and anger. So many emotions swim in them that it takes my breath away.

"I will never be able to put my trust in you unless you tell me who you are."

I exhale, stretching it out as long as I can while I consider what to tell her. All I told Jon was that I was in prison, but I know that isn't going to satisfy Amira. No, she wants to know it all. Every dirty, sordid detail.

"When the virus hit," I finally say. "I was in jail."

I keep my eyes on her, waiting for the moment when she backs away, but all she does is blink. "Go on."

I let out a deep breath. Every inch of me wants to look away. To focus on something else. Anything but the girl in front of me who is begging for answers. The only person I've ever wanted to please in my entire life.

At least since Rachel.

"In two thousand ten I was sentenced to fifteen years in prison. Because of that, my sister was put into foster care." Just thinking the words hurts, but saying them nearly tears me in half. "I never saw her again."

"What happened?"

The inflection in a deaf person's voice is different than a hearing person's, making it impossible for me to know what she's thinking. Is she disgusted? Curious? Ready to toss me out on my ass? I don't have a clue and the expression on her face isn't giving anything away, but the possibilities scare the shit out of me.

"My mom was a junkie, my dad a member of a motorcycle club."

Amira blinks. "Like *Sons of Anarchy*?"

"Nothing that dramatic, but there was still a lot illegal shit that went on. I think the show fueled my ego though, which was already as big as the fucking Titanic. I thought I was invincible. Thought no one could touch me. Not the club, not the law, not my dad. In my mind I was king. The next Jax Teller." I let out a bitter laugh and shake my head. "Or the first, considering he was the figment of some Hollywood asshole's imagination."

"What happened to your sister?" Amira says, pulling me from my own self-loathing.

I shake my head and focus on her eyes. "I was her guardian. Like I said, our mom was a junkie. We had different dads, and hers was never around, meaning I was it for Rachel. When I got arrested, there was no one to take care of her. She disappeared as quick as a puff of smoke on a windy day." I put my fingers to my lips and pantomime someone blowing something away. "November fourteenth, two thousand ten I got sentenced to fifteen years, and poof, she was gone. She was ten years old."

Amira swallows and looks away. It's a like a fucking knife

in my heart, knowing that she can't stomach the idea of even looking at me. "What did you do?"

"Nothing big by prison standards. Drug charges. Possession with the intention to sell. That kind of bullshit. But it was the fact that I ruined my sister's life in the process. That was the real nail in the coffin. Because of me, she was sucked into the world of foster care. I'd been there and I knew enough of what it entailed to realize it would be a death sentence to a ten-year-old girl like her. She was a sweet kid. Never let our bitch mom get to her. Always saw the sunny side and all that shit. I swore I'd never screw her over like Sylvia had—that was our mom. Then I did. And I never forgave myself."

"I sat in prison for almost three years before the virus hit. Hated myself every day and was sure that even if I got out, I would somehow end up right back there, eventually dying inside those bars. Then the virus came. People on the outside started dying. Then people on the inside. The guards brought it in and the virus swept through the place, killing most of us. I sat there in my cell, nearly starving. Most of the guards had stopped coming in—too sick to work—but still I couldn't get out. Then the people around me succumbed. One after the other until I was the only one left on my block. I was damn sure I would die behind bars. Worse, I knew I deserved it. Even as the bodies around me came back, the only thing I could think about was Rachel. How I had failed her. Deserted her. How she deserved better." I let out a deep breath and look away. "Finally, one of the guards came back. Took pity on the poor souls stuck in their cages and let us free. By then most of the world had slipped away, but I knew it was my second chance. And I swore to myself that I was going to do better. The man I was before, he died in prison with all the other assholes. I'm different. I'm better."

I stop talking, biting back the last piece of information I haven't revealed. Not because I don't want her to know—after everything else it doesn't change much about who I am—but because I can't stomach the idea of saying the words out loud. Of revealing to Amira that I went to find Rachel when I got out and what condition she was in. Dead, yes. That was to be expected. But seeing the bites on her and knowing *how* she had died was enough to drown me in my own self-hatred.

Amira blinks a few times and I hold my breath, waiting for her to tell me to get the hell out of her house. She should. She should realize what a danger I am to her. Send me away before it's too late. Nothing good can come of having me around.

"That's it?" she says, finally turning to look at me again. Her expression soft. Understanding.

I shake my head like I don't understand. "Isn't that enough?"

"What about since the zombies? What have you done since then?"

"I told you. I was with a group in Colorado. We were working to get the city cleared out and start over when we found out about the CDC. When we found a guy who was immune, we headed that way."

"I'm deaf, not dumb," she says, taking a step closer to me. "And I know one thing about this new world. There are plenty of groups out there you could have joined up with who wouldn't have given a shit about the CDC or a vaccine or anything else that didn't serve their purpose. Why didn't you look for a group like that? Why choose to stay with a group who was working to move forward?"

It's a question I've never asked myself, but one that makes sense. "Because I wanted to move forward, too. Prove that I'm better than the asshole I was. I still do."

Amira sucks her bottom lip into her mouth, studying me while I wait to find out my fate. When she lets out a deep breath, it's enough to melt away the tension in my body.

"Next time we're out, you have to let me know you're leaving me to fend for myself. I have to know when I need to watch my back."

The guilt that had started to ease comes back full force.

"Shit. I'm sorry, okay. I'm a thoughtless asshole."

The smile Amira shoots me only helps relieve a little bit of the guilt. "You're not an asshole. You're just not used to having a deaf girl around."

"It won't happen again. Okay?"

"That's all I needed to know."

CHAPTER SIXTEEN

AMIRA

Jim is a convict.

The candlelight flickers across the room, giving me just enough light to study the man sleeping next to me. His eyes twitch, but otherwise his face is smooth. Expressionless. Nothing about him is threatening when he's asleep—or even when he's awake, for that matter—but what he told me explains so much about why he's avoided discussing his past.

He shifts and the sheet moves aside, revealing more of the tattoo on his bicep. It's all black, the lines so thick and dark it looks like they've been put there to hide something. Only an inch below it, just under his elbow, is a scar. A red gash that nearly wraps around his arm. I can't imagine the damage a cut like that would have done to him or the violence that must have surrounded it. Did he get in prison? Before? What must his life have been like to encourage someone to do so much damage?

My own life has been filled with nothingness. Until the virus hit, I'd lived a dull existence that consisted of me trying to please my parents. When Jim made the crack about that one cigarette being the only rebellious thing I've ever done, he wasn't wrong. I've always been a people pleaser, and even though I knew my parents loved me, there was a part of me that felt I had to be perfect to earn that love.

A hand touches my arm, and I turn to find Jim's eyes on me. *"What are you thinking about?"*

Like Jim, I've avoided talking about the past. I thought we were doing it for different reasons—because I was hiding from it and he was hiding who he was—but now that I've heard his story, I realize I was wrong. We're both just trying to move on with our lives the best way we can, which sometimes means leaving the past behind.

"Michael." Saying his name hurts worse than anything I've ever done.

"Your brother?"

"We were adopted." I smile through the tears clogging my throat, knowing Jim has already deduced that from the pictures hanging around the house. "Mom and Dad were married for more than ten years before they gave up trying to have their own kids. They brought me home from Nicaragua when I was a little over two years old. I could still hear a little at the time, but it was getting bad." Jim's eyebrows shoot up and I shrug. "I don't remember it, really. My biological parents gave me up, left me at an orphanage run by missionaries. When I came here my new parents bought me hearing aids. It helped for a bit, but by the time I was five my hearing had gone completely."

Jim reaches out like he's going to comfort me or take my hand or something, and my heart leaps with anticipation. When he drops his hand against the bed, my heart drops with it.

"When did you learn sign language?"

"I started almost as soon as I arrived in the states. My hearing loss was a degenerative thing, and my parents knew
120

it would eventually go completely." I turn my eyes to the ceiling when an odd pang shoots through me. "My biological parents rejected me because of it, and even though I knew my new parents would never do that, I always felt like I needed to do everything right. I wasn't a cheap or easy child, and I wanted to make sure I earned the love and money they spent on me."

Jim grips my chin between his fingers, and when he turns my face, we're only inches away from each other. Lying in bed like this, side by side, our bodies are so close that I can feel every breath he lets out, and when his gaze travels down, stopping briefly on my lips, it sends a shiver of pleasure shooting through me.

"I'm sure you were the perfect kid."

"I don't know about that." I want to laugh, to lighten the mood, but with Jim's fingers still gripping my chin and his face so close to mine, it's impossible. The air around us sizzles, and it has nothing to do with the stale air or the Georgia humidity that has settled over the house.

Jim lifts his eyebrows and finally lets go of my chin, giving me a little more room to breathe. *"Name one thing you ever did wrong other than smoke a cigarette behind your garage."*

My laughter shakes the bed. "I'm not perfect."

"Compared to other people, I bet you are." Jim grins. *"Are you avoiding the question because you don't have an answer?"*

"Of course not!" I sink my teeth into my bottom lip while I try to come up with something. "I... In high school, I dated a guy my parents didn't like. We had to sneak around, and a couple times I lied and told my mom and dad that I was spending the night at a friend's house."

"But you spent the night with him instead?"

"We had this special place we'd go to, and he'd set up a tent."

Jim's blue eyes study mine, and I wait for him to laugh. Maybe even tell me I'm an amateur and that he could have really shown me how to rebel.

Instead of giving him the chance to do anything that would even resemble flirting, I ask, "What about you? You must have had a significant relationship at some point."

His brows move up, slowly, his eyes holding mine. *"Are you asking if I was married?"*

Jim being married hadn't really occurred to me—he doesn't seem like the type—but the fact that he jumped to that conclusion says otherwise.

"Were you?"

He nods, still watching me. *"I was."*

For a second, I don't know how to react. He told me about prison, and about his junky mom and his motorcycle club dad, even about his sister. But he never mentioned a wife. Why not?

"You must have been young."

"Twenty." He shrugs. *"It didn't last long."*

"Did you get divorced when you went to jail?"

"It was over by the time I went to jail. She wasn't really concerned about a piece of paper when she slept around on me, so I didn't see the point in filing for divorce."

"So you're still married?" I say before I can think better of it.

Jim just smiles. *"I doubt she's alive, but technically, I guess I am."*

I nod and look away, filing the new information away for later before saying, "How are you feeling?" It was a rough day, and after we got back from getting supplies—and had our little talk—Jim practically passed out.

"Worn out. I think I've beaten the infection, but I still don't have all my strength back. It's going to take a while."

"Don't push yourself," I say. "Now that we have supplies we can take some time to relax. Let you heal."

Jim pulls the covers down and pats his stomach, revealing his firm body. *"Need to fatten myself up. I lost too much weight."*

Yeah, he looks totally emaciated and disgusting. Right.

Heat spreads across my face and I turn away, rolling out of bed and calling over my shoulder, "Might as well start
122

now. You fell asleep before we could eat."

The food we got at the Millers' house is lined up in the closet, and just seeing the rows and rows of nonperishable items causes hope to swell in my chest. We got a nice haul, which should put us in good shape.

I grab a box of protein-packed granola bars off the shelf — peanut butter, my favorite — and a tin of mixed nuts before heading back into the bedroom. Jim is still in bed, his head propped up as he watches me cross the room. With his gaze on me like this, every hair on my scalp prickles in anticipation.

"You need lots of protein." I wave the two items in front of his face, hoping to break the spell between us. "So it's a good thing we found all this stuff. It will keep us going for a while."

Jim frowns, but I ignore it as I plop down on the bed and dig into the box of granola bars.

"You want one?" I ask, holding the wrapped bar out to him.

He takes it, still watching me, but he doesn't open it. *"I wish you'd reconsider leaving."*

"Do we have to talk about this right now? It's not like we can go anywhere at the moment, anyway. You're still too weak. You need more time to recover."

"That's true, but we can take this time to get ready. That way, we'll be prepared when the time comes."

I rip the foil packet open and pull the granola bar out, focusing on the process while I give myself time to think. When I take a bite, the gooey peanut buttery goodness makes me sigh out loud.

"I love peanut butter."

Jim's mouth turns down, but he opens his own granola bar and takes a big bite. He chews, slowly, watching me the entire time.

When he's done chewing, he says, *"Tell me about your parents."*

I almost let out a sigh of relief at the subject change. Instead, I take another bite of the granola bar. When I've swallowed I say, "What do you want to know?"

"Were you close?"

"Yeah. I was pretty dependent on them. Looking back, I think they wanted it that way. They were older and had waited so long to have kids, and the idea of me leaving scared them. Well, at least it scared my mom. Dad was something else." I shrug and roll my eyes. "I went away to college and Mom texted me at least ten times a day. When the virus hit she begged me to come home, so I did. It was only supposed to be temporary, but you know how that turned out."

Jim puts his hand on my knee, and I pretend that no tingles shoot through me. *"Did your mom and brother die from the virus?"*

"Mom went first." I look away even though I won't be able to tell if he's talking to me. The tears in my eyes have distorted everything anyway, so I doubt I'd be able to read his lips. "It took less than two days for the virus to take her out, but none of us got sick for a while." I have to pause to swallow. The granola bar that tasted so good a couple minutes ago has turned to rocks in my stomach at the thought of what happened next. "We still weren't sure it was the end at that point, but Dad couldn't get in touch with anyone to come get the body. She was still here when she turned two days later."

Jim gives my leg a squeeze, but I still don't look at him.

"Dad put a bullet through her head." My gaze moves to the .22 leaning against the wall. That was the gun he used on Mom, and the one I had to use later on Michael. Just thinking about it hurts, so I try not to. "A week later, Michael came down with a fever." I close my eyes when sobs shake my body. "Dad was gone, out getting supplies, and Michael was so sick. I knew what would happen if my brother died. Knew he would turn, too. I prayed. I prayed so hard that he'd get better or that Dad would make it back so I didn't have to deal with it. The thought of having to put a bullet in my brother's

124

head, even if he would already be dead, made me want to die too. Dad was still gone when Michael reached the end." Once again, I glance toward the rifle. "That's what I used to put him down. Every time I look at it, I'm reminded of my brother and the horrible end he came to."

Jim's fingers squeeze my leg, and I open my eyes to find him watching me. The room is dark, only illuminated by the flickering light of the candle, but I swear there are tears in his eyes.

"I'm so sorry."

"I did what I had to do," I say even though that's not how it feels. It feels like I killed my brother.

Jim sits, and his hand slides farther up my thigh. His eyes are still on mine, so intense and searching that it makes me squirm. When he looks at me like this, it's hard to imagine that he could ever do anything violent. Especially not violent enough to send him to prison.

"You're a good man. I'm glad you found me."

Something flickers in his eyes, but he looks away before I can grab hold of it. His gaze instead focuses on the .22. *"You don't have to use that anymore, you know. The carbine we found today would be better. More power, but not the kickback an automatic weapon has."*

I follow his gaze to the .22, but the familiar tightening in my stomach makes me look away. "If I never touched that rifle again, I'd be happy. It was all I had after Dad left, though."

Jim nods. *"There's no reason you have to use it, then. Life is hard enough without dragging painful memories with you. From now on, you'll use the carbine."*

CHAPTER SEVENTEEN

JIM

I really thought telling her about my past would change things, and it has, only it's made things more clear somehow. It was like she needed me to open the doors to our pasts so she could move forward.

"I found her," I say without thinking about it. "After I got out of prison, I went to look for Rachel, and I found her."

Amira's eyebrows shoot up. "She was alive?"

"No." I want to look away, especially with her intense brown eyes focused on my lips the way they are, but I can't. It may hurt to say the words, but I know I need to get them out. "It took some time to track down her foster house, but when I finally got there she was dead. I wasn't surprised, most of the world was dead by that point, but I didn't know how much it would affect me. Knowing how she died."

"What do you mean?"

"She was covered in bites. Like she'd survived the virus only to be attacked by one of the dead. How she survived an attack, I don't know, but she must have fought them off or run away or something. The bites ended up killing her anyway, and then she turned." I let out a deep breath. "But knowing how much pain she must have gone through, and that she'd been all alone in the end, it nearly killed me."

This time when I exhale, I feel lighter. Like saying the words out loud has helped ease some of the guilt I've been carrying. It also hits me for the first time that as much as it hurts, I'm lucky to know what happened to my sister. I don't have doubts about whether or not she's alive. She didn't disappear without a trace. That happens a lot these days, and even though it usually means death, it has to be torture.

Which is what Amira is going through right now.

When I meet her gaze again, I take her hand. "We'll stay for a bit. Wait to see if your dad comes back."

Amira's brows pull together and she frowns. "Why?"

"Because you need closure, and if we can find it, then we should."

I WAKE TO THE SOFT PING OF RAINDROPS HITTING the windows. It echoes through the room, filling the silence with familiarity. The already hot house has gotten warmer as we slept, and the air is now sticky with humidity. And it's only going to get worse. Once summer is in full swing, Georgia will be scorching.

"Fuck I'm hot."

I pull the covers off and lie in the darkness, staring at the ceiling as the rain falls on the house. Next to me, Amira is out cold. Her heavy breathing is just audible over the sound of the rain. I try to will my body to relax, to drift back to sleep, but the heat hanging in the air is too thick. Almost suffocating.

It's too hot to stay inside with all the windows and doors sealed tight all the time. Amira may think it's for our protection, but we're going to end up roasted alive if we don't get some fresh air every now and then.

I slide out of bed, careful not to disturb Amira, and head across the room. A little bit of light shines in when I pull the blanket off the window, but with the clouds clogging the sky, there isn't a lot. It's still early, probably no later than nine o'clock, and even though the rain is light at the moment, the gray sky tells me more is coming our way.

"Now's a good time to get some air moving."

Even though I know my talking won't bug Amira, I glance toward the bed to make sure she's still out. She hasn't moved. When I pull the window open, a breeze blows through the room. It's damp and humid, but cooler and a hell of a lot more refreshing than the stale air clogging the house right now. I close my eyes and let out a sigh as more air blows through the open window.

"Should have done this sooner."

I leave Amira where she is and head out into the main part of the house, opening windows as I go. The wind rushes through the house, airing it out in what feels like seconds. When every window I can find is wide open, I sit at the dining room table and watch the storm clouds roll in. The sliding glass door is open too, and it's so fucking nice to have fresh air that I feel like a new man.

Footsteps enter the room behind me a split second before Amira says, "What are you doing?"

I twist to face her, smiling. "Feels nice, right?"

She shakes her head. "It's dangerous!"

Amira rushes for the open door like she's ready to weld it shut so I can never open it again. I jump to my feet, blocking her. When she tries to push past me, I grab her arms and force her to meet my gaze.

"It's going to be okay. We have to let fresh air into the house. Plus, it was getting hot." I jerk my head toward the open door. "I'm keeping an eye on things."

She shakes her head and tries to step back, but I don't let her go.

"What do you think is going to happen?" I ask.

"A zombie could find us. We don't know how they operate. They could smell us or something."

"They don't have superpowers."

She presses her lips together so hard that they flatten, giving off the impression they've been glued together. "You sure?"

"Trust me."

Something flickers in her eyes when I say it, and last night comes screaming back. The moment when I laid myself bare in front of her, and the look in her eyes that told me she wanted more. Damn. I want it too. Especially now, standing with my back to the door, the cool air sweeping over us. She's so close to me that all I'd have to do is take one tiny step forward and I'd be able to feel all of her.

I let go of her arms and take a step back.

"I trust you," she says.

"Take a seat." I wave toward the chair as I sit back down, and Amira sits too.

Together we watch the storm move closer. The clouds get darker, and a bolt of lightning cuts across the sky. Instantly, the rain gets heavier. It pounds down on the earth like it's trying to drown us all, filling the house with its thundering power.

Amira stands, and even though I don't know what she's doing, I do too.

"This is good," she says as she heads for the garage. "We need the water. Let's put the buckets out."

THE NEXT TWO DAYS ARE OVERCAST, AND THE RAIN comes and goes. It's so loud at times that it keeps me up, but Amira sleeps right through it.

It's been close to two weeks since I ran out of that farmhouse. Everyone else should be long settled in Atlanta, and when I'm alone at night, staring into the darkness, I can't help wondering if I'm an idiot to wait for Amira to be ready. Her father isn't coming back, and I think she knows that. Plus, the longer we stay here, the more likely it is that we're going to run into trouble. We should leave, but I know I can't force her.

As the weeks pass, Amira and I fall into a routine. We play cards and laugh, we eat, we collect and boil water, and we get to know each other. Over those weeks, I get stronger. The cut on my leg starts to bother me less and less, and I put some of the weight I lost back on. When I get back into my routine of pushups and sit-ups, the reality of how much Amira did for me sinks in. The infection took so much out of me that even the simple exercise routine I had in prison is difficult. If I hadn't found this girl, I would have died for sure.

"What were you studying in college?" I ask one day in early June as I haul a big pot of water onto the camp stove.

She crosses her arms over her chest, and I do my best not to focus on how it pushes her boobs up. "Literature."

"Literature? What were you going to do with that?"

"Teach." She shrugs. "I wasn't sure, I just knew I loved to read. It was fun, but the closer I got to graduation, the more I started to worry that I'd made a mistake. Not that it matters now."

She slumps back against the counter and frowns, her gaze moving to the window. Outside, there isn't a single cloud in the sky, and the days have gotten so warm that it's hard to breathe sometimes.

A bead of sweat rolls down the side of my face, and I wipe it away. "It's hot."

"What?"

I turn, realizing I was facing the window. I've gotten better about remembering to keep my lips where she can read them, but there are still times when I forget. "I said it's hot."

"It's going to get hotter."

Her eyes move down, looking herself over. I do my best not to follow her gaze, but it's a tough task. The hotter it gets, the skimpier her clothes become. Right now, the shorts she's wearing are so small that they barely cover her ass, and her tank top is tight. Every time I look her way my

131

imagination goes wild, especially when she's wearing something like this.

"We should go swimming," she says out of nowhere.

I shake my head because I'm sure I didn't hear her right. "Swimming?"

"Yup."

Amira shoves herself off the counter and heads into the other room, leaving me alone with the steaming pot of water and a rock-hard dick.

CHAPTER EIGHTEEN

AMIRA

L et's go," I say, holding my bag of toiletries up. "I'm hot, I probably stink, and I'm not going to lie, you could use some freshening up too."

Jim's eyebrows shoot up. *"You still haven't told me where you plan to go swimming."*

"Can't anything be left to mystery these days?" When he doesn't move, I let out an exaggerated sigh. "Are you going to drive me, or do I have to ride my bike?"

He still looks skeptical, but he flips the camp stove off. *"Let me get my shit together."*

"I'll get the towels!" I call after him.

Jim asks where we're going about a hundred times as we drive down the road, but all I do is grin and point when he needs to turn. I haven't been to the swimming hole since before the outbreak, and even though a childish excitement surges through me at the thought of returning to something that resembles normal, I try to suppress it. Who knows what we'll find. Everything has changed, and I'm not ignorant enough to believe that the apocalypse couldn't have penetrated even this little bubble of happiness.

When I tell Jim to turn onto a dirt road, he gives me a look that says he just might think I'm crazy. Then, when the road ends at the forest line, he looks at me like he suspects I might be leading him out here to kill him.

"Trust me," I say before pulling the door open and hopping out.

Before I move away from the car, I take a deep breath. The scent of nature floods my nostrils. Grass and dirt and fresh air, as well as a dozen different smells that all scream wildlife. No death, though.

I turn to find Jim waiting at the front of the SUV. The AK-47 rifle he found at the Millers' slung over his shoulder and the M1 carbine in his hand, waiting for me to take it.

I skip over to join him, smiling when I take the rifle. "Ready?"

He lifts one eyebrow. *"You tell me."*

"You are going to love this."

He chuckles, and the smile that spreads across his face lights up his blue eyes. Under the bright sun, they sparkle more than ever, and for the first time since we met, a pang shoots through me at the knowledge that I can't hear what that laugh sounds like.

"I'll be your ears." He nods toward the trees. *"You lead the way."*

I take off, ducking through the brush and making my way into the thick mass of trees. Wildflowers have pushed their way up through the layer of dead leaves covering the ground, spreading life into the forest that's even more intense than the green leaves above us. Cloaked mostly in shadows, it's cooler under the protection of the trees. Even in the occasional spot where the sun has broken through the branches, the heat from the rays can't overpower the gentle breeze that fills the space between the trees.

When we reach the end of the forest, I pause to wait for Jim. My heart speeds up, thinking about the possibility of finding my little oasis ruined. It's enough to make me hesitate.

Jim touches my elbow, and I turn. *"What's wrong? You smell something?"*

I shake my head. "No. Let's go."

I let out a deep breath and push myself forward, breaking out of the tree line and stepping into the open meadow. The sun reflects off the pool of water in front of me, sparkling so brightly that I have to squint, but even with my eyes half closed, it's obvious no one has been here in a long time. Maybe not since the last time Michael and I came swimming.

"Tada!" I say, spinning around to face Jim.

"This is probably the best thing I've ever seen." He grins down at me before looking over my head toward the little pool of water. *"How did you know this was here?"*

I turn to face the swimming hole, dropping my bag, towel, and rifle on the ground. "When I was little, my aunt and uncle owned a farm on the other side of the trees. They used to bring me here to swim. Even after they sold the place, we'd come here to swim."

I stop when a million memories slam into me. Bringing Michael here. Teaching him to swim. Watching his smile as he ran and jumped into the water. Then there was Carson, my high school boyfriend. This was our spot, where we'd come on nice days so we could stretch out under the sun. Where we camped and went skinny dipping. So many happy memories took place inside these trees.

Until now, I never really understood what the word bittersweet actually meant.

Jim drops his own bag to the ground next to mine, and I turn to face him when his shirt joins it. He isn't looking at me as he unzips his pants, and the heat that floods my body has nothing to do with the hot summer day.

I tear my eyes away from him when all the memories I'd just been sorting through fade away, leaving behind only the ones of Carson and me. Is that why I brought Jim to this secluded clearing? Here we are, already so attracted to one another. There will be no clothes, no interruptions, and so many possibilities that it makes my head spin.

Jim nudges me, drawing my attention his way once again. He shoots me a grin before taking off running, nothing but a whirl of color as he jumps into the little pool. Water splashes up around him, and then he's gone. Swallowed by the sparkling surface in front of me.

In less than five seconds, his head pops up, bringing with it another splash of water and flailing arms. His smile is so big that it looks like it hurts, and he's waving to me. His lips move too fast for me to catch his words, but I don't need to. He's telling me to join him.

"I'm coming!" I call.

Heat spreads across my cheeks when I pull my shirt over my head, and my eyes are focused on the grass as I drop my shorts. For a second, I consider removing my bra, but since Jim left his boxers on, I think better of it.

He's still grinning and waving when I run for the pond. I jump, like he did, squealing just before I too am sucked under. The water is only slightly colder than a bath, but after the humidity of the day, it's more refreshing than I could have imagined.

I stay down for a few seconds, then kick my feet, blowing all the air out of my lungs when I shoot back up. I surface right in front of Jim, who laughs and grabs my shoulders. When his lips move, it takes a lot of concentration for me to read them.

"This is amazing!"

"I told you."

I grin as I kick away from him and tilt my body back. Forcing all my muscles to relax, I allow myself to float on the surface, weightless and at ease. Letting the sun shine down on my face and warm me from above, the cool water sweeping over me from below. Water laps against my face, tickling my cheeks, and for just a second I'm able to pretend that I'm in

136

the past. Young and carefree. I have my whole life ahead of me and two parents who I know will never leave me alone and defenseless in a world meant for the hearing.

Too soon my body starts to sink, and the fantasy is washed away when cool water sweeps over me. My mouth fills, and I kick my feet, forcing myself up as I spit.

I open my eyes to find Jim standing on at the edge of the pond, washing his hair. Beads of water run over his chest to his stomach, tracing his muscles like the fingertips of a lover. He's bulkier now than he was, and if his body was a distraction before, it's now become a full-blown obsession. Even though it's been weeks since I had to help him get cleaned up and dressed, I can still remember what those muscles felt like. He was sick—probably dying—but it still felt so good to have the warmth of another person under my hands.

Jim dives under, resurfacing a second later and using his hands to rinse all the soap from his hair. When he's finished, he goes under again. This time when he pops back up, he tosses something onto dry land. It only takes two seconds to realize it was his boxers.

"What are you doing?" I call before I can stop myself, my cheeks—and other parts of me—heating from the knowledge that he is now totally naked.

Jim grins as he treads water only six feet away from me. *"Relaxing. You can join me if you want."*

He wiggles his eyebrows, and I actually laugh. This is a side of him I've never seen. We've gotten more comfortable with one another even as the attraction has grown more intense, but he's never flirted with me before.

"I'm good," I say, but a part of me is jumping for joy at the thought of stripping my clothes off. "Thanks."

He shrugs. *"Suit yourself."*

When he leans back and lifts his body so he's floating on the surface of the pond, I turn away.

I swim to the edge and pull myself out so I can get my own shampoo, flushing at the sight of Jim's boxers.

137

When I turn back, he's once again treading water. Watching me as if he's trying to memorize every line of my body.

"What?"

Jim's eyes snap to my face, and he chuckles. *"I'm a man and it's been a long time since I had sex."*

Just the mention of the thing that's been clawing at the back of my mind for weeks sends a shiver shooting through me. But I laugh it off as I turn away, hoping he doesn't recognize the desire in my eyes or see the heat creeping up my cheeks.

Standing on the edge of the pond, I dump a generous amount of shampoo in my hand and work it into my dirty hair. When I turn back, Jim is once again floating on his back, balanced on the surface like a buoy as the sun shines down on him like it wants to highlight every inch of his body for me. It's tough, but somehow I manage to force myself to focus on the task at hand, working my fingers through the strands to untangle them and then massaging my scalp with shampoo. Washing every ounce of filth away. Not thinking about Jim or how naked he is or sex...

Okay. That's a lie. I think about it the whole time I wash my hair, then while I rinse. It's so present in my mind that when I'm finally done, I do everything I can to avoid his gaze as I head back to dry land.

The sun beats down on me, warming my skin, and I turn my face upwards. While the water was nice, lying under the sun and enjoying the utter stillness of this summer day sounds like paradise.

I spread my towel across the grass and stretch my body out on top of it, closing my eyes and allowing the sun to sweep over me. "Be my ears, Jim," I say, not opening my eyes.

A breeze sweeps across the meadow, causing the grass to tickle my arms. Something crawls across my leg and I swat it away as I inhale, savoring the memories these smells bring. Everything has a distinct scent, and this meadow is no different. It's so strong that I can almost feel Carson's lips on mine...

138

A shadow falls over me just as a hand grabs my arm, and I bolt upright so fast that my head slams into Jim's face. He lets me go and grabs his nose, sitting back. Holding it as he rocks back and forth like he's in horrible pain. My heart is pounding so fast I can't catch my breath, and I'm too focused on studying the meadow to worry about him.

Is there trouble? Was he coming to tell me something was wrong?

I scan the area three times before my heart starts to settle down. There's nothing as far as I can tell. That doesn't mean he didn't hear something.

"What's wrong?" I move closer to Jim and grab his arms, forcing his hands away from his face so I can see him.

His blue eyes shimmer when he looks up, and he shakes his head. *"You headbutted me."*

"That's not what I meant." I shake my head and look around again. "Did you hear something?"

Jim wipes the tears from his eyes and rubs the bridge of his nose. *"No. I just wanted to know what you said. I was underwater, and when I came up, I caught the tail end of what you were saying."*

So there's no trouble. He was just trying to get my attention.

"Oh my God." I scoot closer and grab his face between my hands. His stubble rubs my palms, tickling my skin. "I'm sorry. You startled me. Are you okay?"

His mouth opens just a little like he's letting out a groan, and he squeezes his eyes shut. When he opens them, he nods. *"I'm okay."*

Then his eyes move down.

Now that my worry has worn off, it hits me that he is totally naked and I'm halfway there. I'm also practically sitting in his lap at the moment. We're so close to one another that his body heat has overpowered the rays of the sun. Goose bumps cover my skin as his eyes make a path across my body, memorizing every inch. Maybe even filing it away for later...

Dear God, why did I have to think about that?

139

I drop my hands from his face and scoot back as heat moves through me, pooling in my stomach and turning to desire. This meadow always was the perfect place for Carson and me to come. So secluded. So secret.

"This is where I used to come with my boyfriend."

I swallow. Why did I say that? Jim's going to know what I'm implying, and it's only going to add fuel to the fire. We're already teetering on the edge.

"*The one you camped with?*" Jim wipes the remaining tears from the corner of his eye.

"That's the one."

He looks around, studying the area for a second before once again holding my gaze. "*Is this where you lost your virginity?*"

A shiver shakes my body even as I nod, and for the first time, I allow myself to look Jim over. I've seen him naked before, the day I first dragged him into my house, but he was sick and delirious with fever then. Now, he's healthy and fit and just as affected by my nearness as I am by his.

Jim grabs my chin and tilts my face up toward his. "*Did you and this boyfriend go skinny dipping here?*"

I nod, too affected to talk and totally unsure of what I'd say anyway. I'm not sure what I want to happen here. For weeks we've been tiptoeing around this, acting like this attraction doesn't exist even though it's constantly hanging over our heads. But I want him, and I know he wants me. The only question I have to answer right now is: do I think it's a good idea to take the next step here?

The wind blows, and I take a deep breath, inhaling the smells of the forest. Reminding me where we are. Out in the open and vulnerable.

No. It would be foolish to do something like this right now.

I scoot away from Jim, pulling my chin from his grasp so I can look down. "Maybe we should head home." I stare at my hands, so if Jim says anything, I don't know. "We don't want to let our guard down like before."

140

He gets to his feet, and even though I keep my head down, I watch him out of the corner of my eye as he pulls his boxers back on. Once I know he's no longer naked—and therefore less of a temptation for me—I push myself up and grab my own clothes. By the time I'm done getting dressed, Jim is ready and waiting with his rifle and bag. My own things are still on the ground, so I scoop them up, shoving my towel into my bag and throwing the rifle over my shoulder before turning to face Jim.

"Now you're going to look at me?" He frowns. *"What's going on?"*

"Nothing. We got clean and had our fun, but now it's time to get home."

Jim shakes his head and when I try to step around him stops me. *"Bullshit. You made a big deal about trusting each other, so trust me. Tell me what you're thinking."*

"Are you serious?" I let out a deep breath and look away. "You know what's going on here, right?"

He grabs my face and turns it toward his. *"You tell me."*

"I'm attracted to you." I press my lips together and jerk my chin out of his grasp. "We're alone all the time and it's only natural, but that doesn't mean it's a good idea."

"Why not?"

I blink. He has to know all the risks surrounding something like this. I search his face, but nothing about his expression looks like he's playing with me.

"I don't know. Because I could get pregnant, which could turn out to be a very bad thing when we're alone and in the middle of nowhere. Or we could get so distracted that we aren't paying attention to our surroundings and something sneaks up on us. There are a dozen more reasons, all of which I know you are smart enough to understand, so I'm not going to waste my breath saying them."

When I'm done talking, I let out a deep breath and look around. Just to make sure nothing is trying to sneak up on me.

Jim shoves his hand through his hair and stares at the ground. Finally, after a few seconds, he nods and looks up. *"Okay. You're right. It's a bad idea."*

I don't miss the fact that he doesn't even try to act like he isn't feeling this too, which makes walking past him and heading for the car that much more difficult. We're attracted to one another and we've both known it for a while now, but this is the first time we've acknowledged it to each other. At this point, I know it isn't just about us being the only two living people within dozens of miles. There's something real between us, but the timing just isn't right.

If we head to Atlanta and it's as safe as he claims it is, we can explore this thing between us. But going there means giving up on Dad, and even though it's been five weeks now, I'm just not ready to admit he's never coming back. Not yet.

CHAPTER NINETEEN

JIM

The sounds of nature follow us to the SUV, practically taunting us. Birds sing while branches rustle above our heads, and the soft crunch of our footsteps fills the silence in between. Every sound is like a reminder that we are alone in this world. Me with this girl who can get under my skin like no one ever has before yet refuses to take that next step. It's infuriating, but somehow makes her that much more desirable.

She's right, but she's also wrong. Very wrong. People make this work, and we can too. But I'm not going to push her into something she isn't ready for, especially when she hasn't finished grieving. Instead, the best thing I can do is once again work on getting her to agree to head for Atlanta. I've let it go, but it's been weeks now, and sooner or later she's going to have to accept the truth.

In front of me, Amira starts moving faster, inhaling deeply as she goes. Scanning the area like she's afraid something is about to jump out at her. I take a deep breath, but I don't smell anything. Still, something has her spooked, so I jog after her through the forest.

When we step out of the tree line, the SUV looms in front of us. Amira stops after only two steps, lifting her hand and motioning for me to stop as well. She sucks in a deep breath through her nose, blowing it out as she looks around. Her dark eyebrows arched and her brown eyes so big they seem to take up half her face.

I scan the area as I pull the AK-47 off my shoulder, but as far as I can see, there's nothing other than fields and blue skies, and I don't hear a damn sound. Still, Amira hasn't moved.

After a second, she shakes her head. "I don't know where it is. We should go."

I nod even though she isn't looking at me, and we both move. Hurrying toward the SUV, scanning the area. She reaches her side and climbs in, and it isn't until her door is shut that I catch the scent of death. Still, though, I don't see anything.

I slide into the passenger seat at Amira's side, and she exhales the second my door is closed. Neither one of us talks as I put the car in reverse, heading back the way we came.

I'm looking over my shoulder when her hand closes on my knee, squeezing it gently. My foot slams against the brake, and I turn to face the front only to find at least a dozen zombies stepping out of the trees. Right where we just came from.

"Shit."

If I'd listened to my dick, we would have done it right there in that meadow. I wanted to. Sitting there next to her, all that soft, cocoa skin exposed to me. It was almost too much. If it had been up to me, I would have stripped her bare right then and there.

And those bastards could have snuck up on us.

"Go," she says, her hand still on my knee.

I twist in my seat once again, looking out the back as I accelerate. My heart pounding a million miles a minute. When I'm once again on the main road, I don't look back the way we came. I just hit the gas and drive.

My heart rate doesn't slow, and I'm driving too fast to look Amira's way, so I don't know what she's thinking. The only thought going through my mind right now is what a dumbass I am. That could have been disastrous.

The house comes into view, still so far away that it's barely more than a speck, and I slow to a stop as all the dread surrounding me intensifies until it's a million times worse.

Figures dot the backyard, stumbling their way toward the house like they heard a dinner bell and came running. Next to me, Amira shifts to the edge of her seat, staring out the front window with her mouth hanging open like she can't believe what she's seeing. I wring the steering wheel, counting. There are eight of them, at least as far as I can see.

"No." The word is so loud in the cramped car that it makes me jump.

I twist to face Amira, my foot pressed against the brake so we don't move, and grab her arm. When she turns to face me, there are tears in her eyes.

"It's going to be okay," I say, putting my hand over hers. "I'll take care of it so we can get back inside."

Even though it seems like the perfect time to remind her about Atlanta, I resist the urge. We both knew that sooner or later zombies would find her house, but rubbing it in is only going to push her away. And I don't want to do that. I want the opposite. I want her to come to the decision on her own. To realize that leaving isn't betraying her family or being stupid. It's the smart thing to do. There's safety in numbers, and in Atlanta we'd have that.

Amira nods as she turns back to face the front.

I ease my foot off the brake, sliding it over to the gas pedal slowly while I try to figure out how to handle this. Eight isn't bad, but I still don't want to get too close.

145

Thanks to the AK-47, I don't need to, but I have to give it some thought. Gunshots could draw anything our way, but eight is too many for me to risk using my knife. I could make a mistake and end up a zombie snack.

The rifle will have to do.

The closer we get to the house, the tenser Amira becomes. By the time I pull to a stop, she's a statue at my side, staring at the house with eyes so wide they seem to take up half of her small face.

I put my hand on her knee, drawing her attention my way. "I'll take care of it." She nods, and I turn toward my door, but so does she. I grab her arm, stopping her. "What are you doing?" I ask when she twists my way.

"I'm helping." She gestures toward the carbine resting at her feet. "I can shoot."

I let out a deep breath. It's not that I doubt her ability, it's that I want her to stay inside. Where it's safe. Where no zombies will catch wind of her.

"You don't have to. I can handle eight."

"We can handle it together," she says before turning away.

She's out before I am, the carbine held in her hands like she's a seasoned solider, and it's so fucking hot it makes my head spin. I meet her at the front of the SUV, my rifle ready, and together we take aim. We're a good fifty feet away still, and the assholes haven't yet caught wind of us. They probably wouldn't if we didn't fire. In fact, right now there's only one thing stopping me from getting in the SUV and driving away for good, and that's Amira. She isn't ready, and I can't force her to leave.

We take aim, standing side by side, but Amira makes the first shot. The crack of gunfire echoes through the silence, and a zombie drops to the ground. When I squeeze the trigger, the kickback sends the butt of the gun into my shoulder, and in the distance, a second zombie falls. I aim for the one at its side, pulling the trigger again only seconds after my first shot, repeating the process with a third zombie. At my side, Amira

146

does the same, and by the time all eight zombies have hit the ground, my shoulder aches and my ears are ringing. But they're all down.

Amira lowers her gun and turns to face me. "Good job."

The twist of her lips tells me she's biting back her own words, possibly even having doubts about what she's doing here, but she doesn't say anything else before heading back to the SUV.

The silence hanging over us has gotten so intense that it's hard to ignore, and I know that if she doesn't bring it up soon, I'm going to have to. We just fired off enough shots to draw every man and zombie around our way, which means staying here has gotten even more dangerous than it was before. She has to know that.

I'm back in the garage, the SUV parked where it originally was, before either one of us speaks again. Even then it's me.

"Watch my back while I drag the bodies off."

Amira nods, her gaze moving across the yard to focus on the distance. She watches, silently waiting, and I know she realizes anything could be heading our way.

First I'll get rid of the bodies, and then we'll talk.

CHAPTER TWENTY

AMIRA

My heart is pounding so hard as I watch Jim drag the bodies away from the house that it feels like a rock band in my chest. This was bad, and the things it could bring down on us could be even worse. I still hate the idea of leaving, but Jim might be right. The house isn't going to be safe forever.

Jim comes jogging back, stopping about four feet away from where I'm standing, his eyes moving over me like he's trying to figure out what I'm thinking.

"What's wrong?" he asks even though we both know.

"It was a nice day."

I hold his gaze, trying to transport myself back to the swimming hole and how it felt to be there and pretend the world wasn't a big pile of shit. It wasn't long, but the short time we spent swimming and relaxing in the sun made me feel almost whole again.

"At least until the zombies snuck up on us," I say, looking away.

Jim grabs my chin and turns my face toward his. "*It was nice. Being with you is nice.*"

A smile pulls up my lips, but it melts away when a second later the wind blows, bringing with it the scent of death. Happiness isn't meant to last in this world, and the sooner I accept that, the better.

I pull my chin out of Jim's grasp and step back, putting space between his body heat and me. "We should go in."

Jim just nods.

I can see his shadow out of the corner of my eye, following me into the garage. It disappears once we're inside, but his presence is so strong I don't feel alone. I may not be able to hear him, but I can feel him in a way that I would never be able to explain with words.

Back inside, I put my things away and hang my towel up to dry, knowing deep down that I saw my old swimming hole for the last time. Whether or not I leave, it isn't safe there anymore. Probably not anywhere.

I look around the house, the familiarity of it warming me like a hug. My gaze stops on the picture of Michael and me that's hanging above the mantel. Our smiling faces pressed together, so close we're like one person. Without thinking about it, I move closer, my eyes locked on my little brother's face.

His death was the hardest thing I've ever gone through. Worse than Mom. Worse than the day Dad didn't come back and I realized I was really, truly alone. Michael was young and innocent, and he had his whole life ahead of him. He shouldn't have died. Especially not in such a painful, unforgiving way.

Jim slips his hand into mine, lacing our fingers together, and I hold on tight. Like he's the only thing keeping me from falling over the edge of a cliff.

"For years it was just me. The spoiled only child. I was almost fourteen when they told me they planned to adopt again, and I was furious. There was no way I wanted to share my mom and dad with some other kid. They went through with it anyway, and the moment I laid eyes on Michael, I was a goner. He was three years old, but so small that he looked younger. Breakable, even. I loved that kid. Loved the way he could make me laugh no matter how angry I was. Loved when he'd climb up in my lap and put his arms around my neck. Loved when he got in bed with me during thunderstorms."

The tears filling my eyes blur out my brother's face, and no matter how many times I try to blink them away, more come. Soon, they're streaming down both cheeks and dripping onto my shirt, threatening to drown me.

Jim takes his hand out of mine and wraps his arms around me. He pulls me against his chest, and all the emotions I've kept locked inside burst out of me as I sob. My body shaking and my heart breaking into a million pieces.

"I don't want to be alone." My words are probably too distorted for him to understand, but no matter how many times I try to swallow down the sobs, I can't. I can't stop them or the feelings inside me that tell me I'm not alone. Not anymore. I may hurt and miss my family, but I have Jim now. Whether it was God or fate or some other mystical being, I'm not sure, but I know Jim is here for a reason. He found my house in a million-to-one shot, and by some miracle I had the medicine that saved his life. We are meant to be together.

He doesn't let me go until my sobs have subsided, and even then he doesn't release me completely. He keeps his hands firmly on my upper arms as he pulls back, looking down at me with an expression so sweet and caring and utterly beautiful that it almost makes me burst into tears all over again.

"You don't have to be alone. Not as long as I'm here."

I swipe my hand across my cheek, wiping away the tears. "Thank you."

I'VE GOTTEN USED TO SLEEPING NEXT TO JIM. TO having his hand brush against me when he shifts, leaving goose bumps on my skin and tingles moving through my body. I wouldn't wish it away for anything, but right now I feel like I'm being roasted alive. Even though I've given in and allowed Jim to keep the windows open during the day, I refuse to allow it at night, which makes the house hotter than an oven.

The darkness and silence filling the room makes me feel like I'm trapped underwater, but no matter how long I lie in bed, staring up at the ceiling, I can't get my brain to shut off. I replay our time at the water hole and what it felt like to come home and find my yard infested with zombies. Then I flip through the details Jim gave me about his life before and after the virus, and how it felt to have his arm wrapped around me. Different than it was with Carson, somehow. I thought I loved my high school boyfriend, cried for days when we broke up, but that feeling was nothing compared to what's been building inside of me all these weeks.

Being this close to Jim and trying to control the urges in my body has gotten almost as unbearable as the humidity filling the house. I could give in. Throw my resistance aside and turn to him now. Press my lips against his. Even if he's asleep, I know he'd be okay with it. The expression in his eyes is too blatant to ignore. He wants me as much as I want him. If I hadn't stopped things, he would have laid me down in that meadow for sure.

Instead, I slip out of bed, careful to keep my movements quiet as I head into the living room. Walking slowly with my back to the wall the way I usually do. It isn't as dark out here thanks the moonlight shining in through the sliding glass door, illuminating the kitchen floor that looks bare now that the flour has been swept up for good, as well as the bucket of Legos in the living room. With Jim here, I don't need them.

My skin is so damp that my shirt clings to my stomach and I have the urge to yank the sliding glass door open and go outside. It has to be cooler out there. Less suffocating.

But doing that would be too dangerous. The bodies Jim pulled to the edge of the property would make it impossible to know if something was sneaking up on me, and it's so dark that anything could be lurking in the shadows.

Instead of going out, I pull my shirt over my head and lean my naked body against the glass. It's cool against my damp skin and refreshing enough that I let out a sigh. I close my eyes and don't move a muscle.

Air conditioning would be nice. If we went to Atlanta, we'd probably have it. Along with hot showers, a real oven, and a million other luxuries I took for granted before the zombies came and destroyed my life.

CHAPTER TWENTY-ONE

JIM

I jerk awake but open my eyes to total darkness. The heat hanging in the air is intense enough to take my breath away, and the sheets cling to my sticky skin, but the other side of the bed is so empty it feels cold. It only takes two seconds for me to jump to my feet.

Where the hell is Amira?

My brain is still cloudy from sleep when I yell her name, and the second I say it, I realize it's a waste of breath. She can't hear me. Even worse, if she's in trouble, I lost what may have been my only advantage. The element of surprise.

I grab the AK-47 from where it leans against the bed and head across the room, raising it and jerking the door open at the same time. Just like the bedroom, the rest of the house is dark. And so silent it sends a shiver up my spine, but I don't know why. If there was trouble, there would be some noise. Wouldn't there?

I pause just long enough to make sure nothing is going to come running and then move. Through the kitchen and out into the living room, my rifle up and my finger poised over the trigger. The moonlight shines in through the glass door, illuminating the room just enough to help me see, but it takes a couple seconds to figure out what I'm looking at.

Amira stands there in nothing but a pair of underwear, her body pressed up against the glass. Her eyes are closed, and her expression is so relaxed that she almost looks like she's asleep. This doesn't make any sense.

I take one quick look around before lowering my rifle and heading her way. There are no zombies or evil men and, as far as I can tell, no reason for Amira to be standing in the living room practically naked.

When I touch her shoulder, she lets out a squeak and spins around. I had every intention of asking her what the hell she's doing, but the second she's facing me, all rational thought disappears. The light from the moon illuminates her brown skin just enough to make it look like she's standing in a spotlight, and her breasts are on full display. Small and perky and just about the best damn thing I've seen in years.

Her eyes grow wide, and she crosses her arms over her chest.

Before I have a chance to get my brain to work, she says, "What are you doing?"

I shake my head and shove my hand through my hair, and even though her breasts are no longer exposed, I can't for the life of me force myself to look away.

"What are *you* doing?" I say instead of answering.

She frowns, and I can't help wondering if she couldn't read my lips. It's dark, but I thought there was enough light for her to see me.

I open my mouth to repeat my question just as she says, "I was hot."

What?

I blink and shake my head, and out of nowhere Amira starts laughing. Only it's different than her normal laugh,

156

which is loud and carefree. This is a nervous sound. So awkward and unsure that it doesn't match her personality at all.

"It was so hot in the bedroom that I couldn't sleep, so I came out here." She shakes her head but won't look directly at me, which makes it impossible to respond. "The glass was cool."

That's the moment that I remember waking up in a pool of my own sweat, the sheets stuck to me. With the door closed, the bedroom is almost unbearable. Out here, though, it's easier to breathe.

She's still staring at the floor, so I grab her chin and turn her face toward me. "It's cooler out here. Sleep on the couch. I'll stay awake and keep watch."

She tilts her head to the side and her arms loosen, but she keeps them crossed. Every inch of me wants her to lower her arms so I can get another look at her body. Better yet, I want to lay her down and explore every inch of her. But that moment at the swimming hole comes back, and I know it wouldn't work. Not right now, anyway. The timing isn't good. It's too dangerous.

"You sure?" she says, bringing me back to present. "Aren't you tired?"

I'm exhausted, but with my blood this close to boiling point, there's no way I'll be able to sleep. At least not until I can get the image of her out of my mind.

"I can sleep later," I say out loud.

After a few second, she nods.

When she grabs her shirt off the floor and pulls it back on, I don't bother holding in my groan of disappointment. It's not like she can hear it, and even if she could I wouldn't care. She knows I want her, just like I know she feels the same way. My self-control is only going to last so long, though.

Amira stretches out on the couch, and I sit on the floor next to her. Every move she makes has me more aware of her nearness, and every breath she lets out sends heat moving through me that has nothing to do with the warm evening.

Damn. There's a good chance I'm never going to be able to calm down enough to sleep.

WHEN I CRACK ONE EYE, THE SOFT LIGHT STREAMING in through the sliding glass door nearly blinds me. Amira's heavy breathing fills the room, so close to my head that it feels like she's pressed right up against me.

My back aches, so I shift, trying to find a better position on the floor. It isn't until my rifle hits the ground that I realize I dozed off. Shit.

My eyes fly open, and I look around, my heart pounding against my temples and my blood roaring in my ears. Through the sliding glass door I can see the empty yard and the fields in the distance, as well as the dark clouds filling the sky. It's later than I thought it was, meaning I've been out for a while.

I push myself up off the floor, groaning when my back pops. On the couch, Amira shifts, but she doesn't open her eyes. One toned leg hangs over the side of the couch, and her tank top has ridden up, revealing her flat stomach. Against the cream-colored couch her skin looks even darker, but just as soft and welcoming.

Kneeling at her side, I take the liberty of running my hand up her arm. Telling myself it's because I'm trying to wake her. Not because I want to touch her so badly that it physically hurts.

She groans, and her eyes flicker open. They search the room for a moment before landing on me, and when she smiles, a grin stretches across my own face.

"Hey," I whisper even though I know the tone of my voice doesn't matter. "It's going to rain."

She pushes herself up off the couch, pulling her tank top down to cover her stomach and revealing more cleavage in the process. "We should put buckets out."

She isn't looking at me, which is why I don't respond. Not

because I'm too focused on the swell of her breasts to get any words out. At least that's what I tell myself.

It isn't until she nudges me with her elbow that I tear my gaze away from her cleavage, and by then all the blood in my body has changed course.

"Seriously?" She lifts her eyebrows.

"I'm a man, and you are fucking gorgeous first thing in the morning."

Pink spreads across her cheeks, and she gets to her feet, looking away. "I should get dressed so we can set up the buckets. We need the water."

"Or you could stay the way you are." Her back is to me and she's already across the room, so there's no way she caught the words, but even if I'd held them at gunpoint, I couldn't have forced them to stay inside.

I stay where I am, blowing out a breath and trying to rid my body of the sexual frustration. It doesn't work. It's almost impossible getting even a few minutes to myself these days, which means things have passed the point of being painful. Even as a teenager, I wasn't this repressed.

Something pings against the glass at my side, and I turn just as a second drop of rain slams into the door. More follow, and the sound echoes through the house like the beat of a drum. It takes seconds for the rainstorm to morph into a downpour, so thick it blocks out my view of the field and turns the outside gray.

"Wow."

Amira stares out the window with her mouth practically hanging open. She's dressed in a tiny pair of shorts and the same tank top. No bra.

"Shit. She must be trying to torture me." I get to my feet and turn to face her. "We should grab those buckets. I'd hate to miss our chance to collect water."

"Yeah." She heads for the garage.

I follow, grabbing the AK-47 on my way by.

Amira stands with a five-gallon bucket in each hand while I lift the garage door. Next to her, six more sit on the floor. With this downpour, it should take less than a minute for those buckets to be full.

The second the door is up, she charges out into the storm. She's soaked before she's taken two steps, but she doesn't hesitate. Amira sets the buckets down and heads back for more, but I'm frozen in place yet again. Staring at her like a hormonal teenager. Her shirt is so wet it's like a second skin, and her shorts aren't much better. Every curve is showcased, begging to be admired and caressed.

"Holy shit. I have to do something about this."

I don't snap out of it until Amira is running out into the rain with two more buckets. I grab the four remaining buckets and head out after her. The drops are big and fat, and they pound down on my head like they're trying to pummel me to death. They also drip into my eyes and make it nearly impossible to see a damn thing.

When I blink, my vision clears just enough to see the buckets Amira set down. I put mine next to them and take a step back, bumping right into her. She laughs and grabs my arm, forcing me to turn to face her. Even in the middle of the pounding rain, her smile lights up the world. I could stare at it all day.

I don't think about it when I grab her hips and pull her against me. Her little body fits so perfectly against mine that it takes my breath way. She looks up, blinking as rain drips into her eyes, and every inch of me wants to kiss her.

She doesn't say anything as she holds my gaze, but even in the middle of the downpour, the conflict in her eyes is as clear as day. Her hands move up my stomach and over my chest, stopping on my shoulders. Her dark eyes holding my gaze as she, too, fights against this attraction.

Fuck this. I'm done fighting with myself.

I lean down, holding her gaze, praying she doesn't tell me no but giving her the chance if she wants to stop me. Her tongue darts out, running across her already wet bottom lip, and I lean forward.

My mouth is less than an inch from hers when movement

catches my eye.

I shove her behind me as I spin around, turning so fast that I nearly lose my balance. My rifle is in the garage, but thankfully I have a knife tucked in my belt. Rain pours down on my head as I pull my weapon, and a figure comes into view, moving toward us through the sheets of rain.

"Back!" I yell, pushing Amira toward the garage.

The man seems to materialize in the blink of an eye, stepping from the rain with his knife already drawn. He dives for me, jabbing his blade in my direction, but I duck out of the way. When I spin around, he's already turned back to face me, but before he can make his move, I tackle him. We go flying, hitting the driveway so hard that it forces a grunt out of both of us. I'm on top, but he isn't fazed enough to stop fighting. He kicks his legs, and his knee makes a direct hit. Agony, red and fiery, spreads through my groin, making me immobile as I curl in on myself.

CHAPTER TWENTY-TWO

AMIRA

The rain is so thick that I can't tell which figure is Jim and which one is the other man. Or if the man is actually a man at all. They roll around on the ground, struggling for a minute, and next thing I know, one is hunched over in a ball while the other is getting to his feet.

Jim is okay.

That's all I can think when the man stands and turns my way. Only it isn't Jim.

"No!"

I run for the garage, my heart thumping against my eardrums with every step I take. If the man is following me, I don't know, just like I don't know if he's fired a gun and killed Jim, because I can't hear a damn thing that's happening.

The rain disappears the second I'm in the garage, but water still runs down my face and into my eyes. I wipe it away as my gaze flies from side to side, searching for the rifle.

The second I set my sights on the AK-47, I dive for it. Somehow I end up on my stomach, but I push myself up and scramble forward on my hands and knees. My fingers wrap around the stock, and then the rifle is in my hand. Fingers wrap around my ankle and my heart pounds harder. I kick and grunt and somehow manage to roll over, already aiming the gun. My finger is poised above the trigger and my arms are steady despite the tremors moving through me.

My finger twitches, but I pause just long enough to make sure the person behind me isn't Jim. When steely brown eyes meet mine, nearly hidden behind the dark hair plastered to the man's face, I pull the trigger.

A jolt radiates through me with the kickback, and red sprays across the pale gray cement of the garage floor. The man hits the ground, falling on his face right next to my feet. My arms are trembling so much that the rifle drops in my lap. I can still feel the force of the shot roaring through me, and it only gets worse when a crimson pool of blood spreads across the floor.

This is the second time I've had to kill a man since Jim showed up.

Jim.

My heart stutters in my chest, and I gasp for breath as I tear my gaze away from the man in front of me, staring out into the pouring rain. Praying for movement. Jim's form is still crumpled on the ground, but he isn't still. He shifts like he's trying to get to his knees, and my heart goes crazy.

Is he shot? Cut? What's wrong?

I'm up in a second, charging back out into the rain. My feet slide and I go down, my knee banging into the cement so hard it makes my teeth slam together. I keep going. Crawling. Pulling myself forward even though every move makes the throbbing in my knee worse.

"Jim!" I scream his name so loudly that I can almost imagine I hear it.

He looks up, his face contorted in pain as water drips down his face.

"Are you hurt?" His lips move, but I can't catch the words, so I grab his chin and jerk his face toward me. "Again! Are you hurt?"

"Bastard kneed me in the balls."

I freeze, searching his eyes as I try to make sense of the words. He isn't shot. He's okay. When it finally sinks in that he's going to be okay, all I can do is burst out laughing.

Jim says something I don't catch, but I don't need to. He's probably cussing me out for laughing or telling me how much it hurts. I deserve whatever he's throwing at me, but I can't make myself stop laughing.

"I'm sorry," I say, throwing my arms around him. "I'm just so relieved. I know it hurts, but I thought you were shot."

Jim pulls back. *"If you had balls you'd understand."*

I laugh harder, my shoulders shaking as rain water runs over my head.

The second Jim slams his lips against mine, though, the laughter disappears.

His hand moves up my back as he pulls my body flush against his, and I can feel every muscle in his chest. Every hard plane and contour. Every breath he lets out as the rain falls down on us and his mouth devours mine.

My hands move up his arms to his face, and the stubble of his beard prickles at my palms. He slides his tongue across mine, sending tremors of pleasure through me. In his arms I feel small but secure. Protected and safe, and exactly where I was always meant to be.

Jim pulls back when a bolt of lightning cuts across the sky. I gasp for air, only to get a mouthful of rain. He gets to his feet as I spit the water out, pulling me with him. Dragging me back toward the house.

The second we're in the garage, he grabs my face between his hands and kisses me. Pressing my back against the SUV. Exploring my mouth with his tongue. It makes my head spin, knowing how much he wants me. Feeling the heat of him against me and knowing that the same heat is moving through me.

I run my hands up his stomach, under his shirt, feeling his hard chest. The last time I touched him, he was delirious with fever, but his skin is just as hot under my palms now as it was then. His lips move against mine in a different rhythm, almost like he's saying something, but I have no idea what it is. I just know that I don't want to stop.

"We should shut the garage," I say between kisses. "Go inside."

Jim's lips move faster, his tongue sweeping over mine as his head bobs. He slides his hands down my face and over my neck to my chest, and when they cup my breasts, I gasp. My legs tremble and threaten to give out.

"Jim." I don't even know why I'm saying his name.

He pulls back, giving me a second to catch my breath, but doesn't move to shut the garage door. Instead he looks me over, his blue eyes sliding down my body so slowly that it sends shivers shooting through me. I press my back harder against the SUV as I prepare myself for the primal desire flashing in Jim's eyes.

When he turns away, I can't move. All I can do is watch as he drags the body out of the garage, leaving the man in the middle of the driveway. Water drips from Jim's hair and clothes when he rushes back inside. In seconds he has the garage door down, plunging us into total darkness.

I stay where I am as my heart beats harder, waiting for Jim to find me. The SUV is cool against my back, and drops of water run down my face and arms. My clothes are glued to my body. I can feel every breath I let out and every beat of my heart, can smell the rain and the dirt and all the other familiar scents of the garage, but otherwise I'm cut off. No sound and no vision.

It makes the anticipation so intense that my legs start to tremble.

Strong hands grab my hips and pull me forward. Muscles and heat wrap around me as those same hands slide up my sides, taking my shirt with them. I move like I'm in a trance, lifting my arms over my head so he can take off my shirt.

166

Then hot lips brush against my shoulder, my chest, my neck, Jim's facial hair tickling me before his lips finally devour mine. Fingers trail down my sides as soft as a feather, slipping into the waistband of my shorts. They move the wet fabric down, peeling it from my body, and lips follow. They forge a trail down my neck and over my chest, the scratchiness of his beard adding to the sensation as he pauses to worship each one of my breasts before continuing his trek.

When my shorts are finally on the floor, those same strong hands lift me. I wrap my legs around Jim's waist and my arms around his neck and hold on for dear life as he starts walking. His mouth working mine with each step. His lips moving like he needs my kisses to live.

The door opens, and then we're inside and I suddenly can see the man who has me. Can see his piercing blue eyes as he lays me out on the living room floor. I watch as he looks me over, his hands following the same journey his eyes take, over my breasts and stomach. Under his touch, my skin heats until I feel like I'm going to burst into flames. The air in the house is hotter than ever, and it's only going to get warmer.

His wet shirt is plastered to his chest. Drops of water drip from his clothes and hair onto my bare skin as he moves his way back up, his fingers running over me, pale against my dark flesh. He pulls back long enough to yank his shirt over his head, his eyes holding mine as he tosses it aside, and then he's back on me. His lips moving over mine.

Jim's shorts are wet when I wrap my leg around his hips, grinding against him. Gasping into his mouth when I feel how much he wants me. His hands grip my butt, pulling me closer. Moving faster.

When he finally pulls away, I can't get his pants off fast enough. The already stuffy house is an inferno, and Jim's skin is damp under my hands. He kicks the wet fabric aside, rolling me onto my back. Kissing me while his hand slides over my chest and moves between my legs. I gasp again when he teases me, opening my eyes to find him watching me closely. His own eyes filled with desire.

"I want you," he says, his gaze moving down my body.

"Yes."

The word is barely out before Jim is between my legs, sliding into me.

WATER RUNS DOWN THE GLASS IN A CONSTANT stream, while outside the storm rages on, shaking the house around us. A brilliant bolt cuts across the sky, and less than a second later the walls around us shake. Thunder like that always fascinated me as a kid. Knowing there was something out there so loud it could make the house around me tremble. Like Mother Nature was putting on a rock concert.

Jim runs his fingers down my bare spine, and a shiver moves through me.

Today I killed a man. Shot him without hesitating. Took a life like I am God and have the right to decide who lives and dies. Until the end of my time on this earth, I will remember the cold expression in that man's brown eyes.

It should be a horrible day, and even though thinking about it leaves a sick feeling in my stomach, that man's death can't overshadow what happened with Jim and me. More than that though, it has me wondering what else could happen. If we go to Atlanta and there really is a wall around the city, if it really is safe like Jim claims it is, we could have a real life. Together. The possibilities are so endless that it takes my breath away.

But to do that we have to leave, which means giving up on Dad. It's been weeks now. Do I really think he could still be out there? Do I really believe he might be able to make it back here?

No.

My stomach clenches, but I can't ignore the brutal truth any longer. Whatever happened to Dad, it had to have been big to keep him away. He wouldn't have left me otherwise.

Jim shifts, and I glance his way just long enough for the pain in my stomach to ease. This man found me for a reason.

He showed up right when he needed me, but also at the exact moment that I needed him.

"I think you were right." I keep my eyes on the glass door in front of me. Watching the rain fall from the sky. "About Atlanta being the right place to go, I mean. But the thought of leaving and giving up on my dad..." My throat tightens so much that the words get stuck, and I shake my head.

That's the tough part. The part that causes tears to spring to my eyes.

Jim moves, twisting so he's stretched out next to me on the floor, his naked body flush with mine. Even in the dim light of the living room, he takes my breath away. I run my fingers over his bicep, tracing the dark lines of his tattoo. Never in my life would I have thought I'd find tattoos sexy, but on Jim they work. Just like the longer hair and the stubble that gives off the impression that he's just woken up from a long night of partying. All of it, the scars included, work together to create the man in front of me, and every inch of him, inside and out, is magnificent.

His lips move, and I pull my gaze away from his bare chest so I can focus on the words. "...this is scary, but we can leave your dad a note. If he comes back, he'll be able to follow us to Atlanta."

"That's just it." I swallow as the words I've been working to avoid bubble up. Getting them out is one of the hardest things I've ever had to do, but I know I need say it once and for all. "I've known for a while now that he isn't coming back. As long as I was here, though, I could pretend it wasn't true. If we leave, it will be like saying goodbye to my family for good."

Jim's mouth tightens like he's trying to decide what to say.

Whatever it is, I don't want to face it right now, so I turn my gaze back to the door. "It's really coming down out there."

There are times like this when being deaf is nice. I can hide from things in ways that hearing people can't.

169

Block out the world and pretend it isn't falling apart around me. That's what I tell myself, anyway.

Jim touches my arm, but I shake my head and keep my eyes on the rain. The second time he does it, I almost turn.

He doesn't touch my arm a third time. Instead he grabs my chin and forces me to turn to face him. *"We need to talk about this."*

"I don't want to talk about it. Not right now. You need to give me time to absorb my decision."

I try to yank my chin out of his grasp, but he doesn't let up. *"Time has run out. That's what I'm trying to tell you. That man came from somewhere, and so did the others we killed. There's a good chance there are more where they came from. We should get out of here sooner rather than later."*

He's right, and dammit I hate that he is. "When?"

"In the morning?"

It's early afternoon now. Leaving in the morning won't give me a ton of time to pack up and say goodbye to my home, but I'm not sure there's ever enough time to prepare for something like this.

"Fine."

He finally allows me to pull my chin out of his hand, and I go back to watching the rain. Not moving even when my stomach growls. We should have lunch, but I can't make myself go into the kitchen. If I make food, then we'll eat it, and before long dinner will be done and it will be time to start packing up. Then it will be time to get some sleep, and before I know it, the sun will be up and we'll be on the road. Once that happens, this chapter of my life will be over. For good. The odds of me ever coming back to this house are slim to none.

Jim runs his hand down my back again, and I force myself to meet his gaze. He isn't looking at me, though, and I can't help thinking that he's trying to give me some privacy to process my emotions. Which is nice.

When I'm finally able to stand, Jim does too. He heads into the bedroom, and I follow. We get dressed in silence, me with my back to him, and when I turn to find him loading our food into a box, I have the urge to climb under the covers and pull them over my head.

Instead, I head over to the wall of pictures and look them over. Trying to memorize the faces of Mom, Dad, and Michael. I should take a picture, but which one?

I study them all, starting with Mom and Dad on their wedding day and moving across the room until I come to our most recent family photo. We're all smiling. Happy. Oblivious to what's about to sweep the country and destroy our lives. It's a nice memory, even if I'll never be able to forget how horribly painful the end was.

I pull the picture off the wall and lay it gently on the bed before heading into the closet to help Jim.

"IT SHOULD TAKE US ONLY A DAY TO GET THERE. Maybe more if we run into trouble." Jim's lips tighten, and he doesn't look at me as he shoves the box of food into the back of the SUV. *"Hopefully, that doesn't happen."*

A silly statement, and we both know it. There will be trouble, but the question is, *what kind?* Zombies we can handle better than people, assuming the horde isn't too big. Driving over them, driving past them, going around them. All three are options. People, however, can shoot at us. Leave traps. Do things even more terrifying than being ripped apart by sharp teeth would ever be. Which is saying a lot.

"You know where we're going?" I ask instead of bringing up all the things that could go wrong.

Jim nods as he turns to face me. *"I already have our trip mapped out on the atlas. Thankfully, your dad had one packed in the car."*

"He didn't like to rely solely on technology." Which saved us. If only it had saved him.

"Lucky for us," Jim says, practically echoing my thoughts.

We stand in the garage, staring at each other silently for a few seconds before he turns and shuts the back of the

SUV. The sun has gone down, and I know we need to get some rest, but that just brings me one step closer to leaving, and I'm not sure I can face it. The outside world is dangerous and unknown now, but even more so for a person like me. I can't hear when someone or something sneaks up on me, and that makes me so vulnerable it's terrifying.

Jim crosses the room so he's standing in front of me and puts his hands on my shoulders, giving them a squeeze. I look up, meeting his serious gaze. His blue eyes sparkle in the dark room, silently asking me if I'm okay. Or maybe trying to reassure me that I will be okay. He'll be with me every step of the way. He'll be my ears when I need them. I can trust him.

"Promise me this is going to turn out okay."

Jim nods. *"I promise that I will do everything I can to make sure you get to Atlanta in one piece."*

He could have told me a lie. Promised we'd be okay forever. Acted like he had control over the future and anything we might face out there. But he didn't, and for some reason the fact that he didn't lie makes me feel better.

"We should get some sleep."

I take his hand in mine and pull him into the house.

CHAPTER TWENTY-THREE

JIM

Amira's heavy breathing fills the room, but I can't make my mind shut down long enough to fall asleep. The heaviness of her life weighs on me. It's even worse than how I felt back at that damn farmhouse. When I ran out into the dark night, I knew I'd done everything I could to keep my friends alive. Knew it would probably mean my death. But things are different with Amira. I want her to survive, but at my side. I don't want to have to say goodbye to her, and I hate how vulnerable that makes us both.

When morning comes, I wake from a sleep that was neither deep nor restful. I roll out of bed, knowing that I should be exhausted after a night of floating in between consciousness and dreams, but I'm too amped up. Too ready to get moving.

The rain finally stopped sometime while we slept, and outside the sky is bright orange. The sun has just begun to pop its head over the horizon. I find Amira in the kitchen, staring out the window and into the backyard. The bright early morning sun reflects off the tears on her cheeks, making me freeze halfway across the room. Her sobs are silent, and I stay where I am for a few seconds, watching the steady stream that slides down her cheeks.

This girl is quite possibly one of the strongest people I've ever met, but it wasn't until this moment that it hit me just how much I've come to care about her. And in such a short time.

When the world ended, I knew I was given a second chance for a reason, and ending up at Hope Springs made me more determined than ever not to waste it. Meeting Jon and Ginny, seeing what could rise out of the ashes of this world, it was even more of a wakeup call. Good things can still happen for people.

For me?

No. Even after all the changes in the world, I couldn't believe that I deserved what those other people had found. So I ran out of that farmhouse, trading my life for theirs but knowing it was the right thing to do. It was my purpose.

Then Amira saved me, and now all of that has changed. She is my purpose. Just looking at her makes my heart swell in a way it never has before. I didn't know a person could feel like this so quickly, and maybe during normal times they can't, but I do know that this thing inside me isn't going to disappear.

I force my legs to move, crossing the room until I'm at Amira's side. She startles when I stop next to her but doesn't move to wipe away the tears. I cover her hand with mine, giving it a squeeze.

"I'm ready," she says after a second, turning away from the window.

The tears are still on her cheeks, shimmering against her dark skin.

Gently, I wipe them away, running my thumb first down one cheek and then the other. "We'll be okay."

174

All we have to do is grab our bags before we head to the garage.

Unlike the other times we left the house, we don't bother pulling the garage door shut behind us, and Amira doesn't have to tell me which route to take. She holds the atlas in her lap just in case, but I have most of the trip memorized. I've stared at the map so many times over the last few weeks, making sure that I know exactly which way to go. That way, when she was ready, all we'd have to do is pack up and head out. Now that it's here, I'm not sure if the tightening in my stomach is from excitement or fear.

The silence is heavy as we drive. I glance over at Amira, who is staring out the window at the passing fields, wishing I could talk to her better while in the car. She can't hear me unless I'm facing her, and I can't do that while I drive.

We've only gone a few miles when I make the first turn, and it doesn't take long before a town comes into view. Even from a distance, I can tell that a lot of it has been burned to the ground, and the closer we get, the more my stomach tightens.

I don't know why I'm uneasy, but I slow the car anyway, pulling to a stop when we're still more than a football field's length away from the outskirts of town. The first few buildings are nothing more than charred skeletons, and even though some are still standing, I can see more remains in the distance.

"This could be bad," I mutter, tapping my fingers on the steering wheel.

"What's wrong?"

I turn to face Amira, frowning. "I just have a bad feeling. I can't put my finger on it."

She mimics my frown as she turns back to face the front, narrowing her eyes like if she looks hard enough, she'll be able to see into the past and figure out what happened here. Which is dumb. We both know what happened here. Zombies happened here. Just like everywhere else.

Still, I can't ignore the uneasiness in my gut.

"Do you want to go back?" she asks, still looking out the window. "Find another way around?"

I shake my head while I grab the atlas off her lap, but it only takes me a few seconds to realize that backtracking would add about thirty miles to our trip. Which means we'd struggle to make it all the way to Atlanta on just this one tank of gas.

"No." I look up to meet her gaze. "I think I'm making a big deal out of nothing."

Amira nods. "Okay."

"You think I should just go through the town?" I don't mean for it to come out like a question, but her answering nod makes me feel better.

I toss the atlas aside and put the car back in drive, gripping the steering wheel like I'm trying to crush it as I ease the gas pedal down. "Here we go."

The silence returns, each of us lost in our surroundings as we reach the outskirts of town. We pass the first few shells of former homes before I see anything else that causes me alarm. Bodies. Piled on the side of the road and burned. The charred remains send a shiver down my spine, but it still could be nothing. If they're zombies, it would make sense that whoever lives here burned the bodies.

We pass a house that has *The Watchers* spray painted across the wall, and Amira tenses. She scoots to the edge of her seat, and I slow. Her eyes are huge. Twice their normal size and shimmering. I follow her gaze to just past the house, where a few cars sit on the side of the road. Like the house, *The Watchers* is painted across the side of each one.

"No." She shakes her head.

I slow even more until I'm moving no faster than a turtle. Is she telling me to go back?

I touch her leg, and when she turns to face me, there are tears shimmering in her eyes.

"What's wrong?" I ask. The tension in my stomach has reached a point so severe that I'm pretty sure I'm going to throw up, and my heart is pounding faster than a speeding

176

train.

Amira nods out the front window, her eyes still on me like she can't stand the thought of seeing it again. "My Dad. That's his car."

Ice coats my insides as I look back out the front window. "Which one?"

"The green truck."

I want to believe that she's mistaken, but the second I set eyes on it, I know she isn't. The color is too unique. Somewhere between teal and emerald green, it reminds me of a peacock's feather. I've never seen any other truck like that.

"He was so close." Her voice is quiet. Like she can barely get the words out.

My hands tighten on the steering wheel. "I should turn around."

When a man steps out from between two houses, I freeze with my hand halfway to the gearshift. Others come out behind him, and I know my chance is lost as more and more men step into view, following the others to the center of the street. Blocking our way. They're all armed, and the arsenal in their possession is so powerful and diverse that it would make an army jealous.

"Holy shit." The words are out before I can stop myself, and I turn to look at Amira, only to find her shoulders shaking with silent sobs.

CHAPTER TWENTY-FOUR
AMIRA

I can see Jim's mouth move out of the corner of my eye, but I can't tear my gaze away from the sight in front of me so I can read his lips. He probably isn't talking to me anyway. If I had to guess, I'd say he's swearing up a storm. Maybe calling himself dumb. Blaming himself for the situation we're in. Who knows? Not me, and right now I can't focus on anything other than the men in front of us and the pain inside me every time I think about my dad's truck sitting just fifteen feet in front of us.

The men blocking the road are so armed it looks like they're heading off to war. Guns I don't recognize well enough to give names but instinctively know are automatic. Meaning they could take us out faster than Jim would ever be able to slam his foot on the gas pedal.

Which is probably what happened to Dad. The words painted across the truck can't cover up the little holes lining the side, or the broken windshield. So this is why he never came back. I thought I'd never find out what happened to him. Now that I have an idea, I think I prefer living in ignorance.

Jim shifts, looking from side to side like he's trying to figure out how to escape. The burned-out houses lining the road make it impossible to go around the group, though, and while going in reverse may be our best option, it isn't going to stop the men in front of us from opening fire.

We're boxed in. Trapped. About to meet a horrible end. I knew it was going to come at some point, I just wish I'd had a little more time with Jim before it happened.

The man at the front of the pack—the one who is obviously calling the shots—waves his arm above his head as he flashes us a smile that sends a shudder shooting through me. His mouth moves like he's calling out to us, but my brain isn't focused enough to be able to read his lips.

I tear my gaze away from the road long enough to focus on Jim's face when he touches my leg. *"This is some bad shit."*

I'd laugh if I weren't scared out of my mind.

"What do we do?"

Jim jerks back a little, and I take a deep breath. Trying to calm myself. No sense shouting at him.

"I don't know." He looks through the front window, wringing the steering wheel like he's trying to choke someone. He doesn't look back the next time his lips move, and I take that to mean he's talking to himself.

"Drive through them?" It's the only thing I can think of, but even I know what a long shot it is. "Make them think we're getting out, then hit the gas when they move closer?"

Jim turns his face toward me, keeping his eyes focused on the front. *"If they move closer. Even then they're likely to shoot."*

He has a point. They may not come up to the SUV at all. They could open fire from where they are and kill us before we have a chance to do anything else.

"Can you read his lips?"

I nod as I turn back to face the road, focusing on the man

who is once again talking.

"…*nice and easy. Weapons down and arms up.*"

"He wants us to get out," I say, still watching the man who hasn't shut up. "He says we should open the doors nice and slow, and put our weapons on the ground. He wants to see our hands in the air."

When I turn back to face Jim, my gaze moves past him to the other side of the street, stopping on the body of a woman who's strung up on a fence. Or what's left of her, anyway. She's naked, which tells me she wasn't a zombie when they killed her. *The Watchers* is spray painted in big, capital letters on the house at her back. It's a safe bet the men in front of us are the Watchers, and I have a strong suspicion that getting riddled with bullets would be a reasonable alternative to letting them get their hands on me.

"I'd rather die than let them have me."

Jim's mouth turns down when he looks my way, but he nods. *"Follow my lead."*

When he turns back, he lifts his hands like he's surrendering. I do the same, trembles of terror moving through me like an earthquake. In front of us, the leader waves, but Jim and I don't move. Here's where we find out what they're going to do. Either they shoot or they head toward the truck.

The leader raises his rifle, and my body stiffens. A second goes by before he waves to the men behind him, his gun still pointed at us. Four men, two from each side, jog our way while the rest of them hold their position. Guns pointed at us. Fingers on triggers. Ready and willing to fire if necessary.

I hold my breath and wait. Without looking his way, it's impossible for Jim to tell me what he's planning, and right now he's too focused on the street in front of us. As am I.

The four men split up when they reach the front of the SUV, two heading toward the driver's side while the other two move to mine. I tap my foot harder with each step they take, unable to hold still. Jim is stiff at my side. Our arms still in the air.

Jim doesn't move until the men are right next to us. His hands go down, one throwing the SUV into drive while the other grabs my head. He forces me down, his hand gripping my skull like I'm a basketball and he's trying to dunk me through a net. I'm staring at the floor when the car flies forward, the momentum pushing my ass back against the seat. I try to sit up, but Jim's hand tightens on my head, making it impossible.

The SUV jerks like we hit someone or something, and my shoulder hits the door when we veer to the right. We keep moving as the tires thump over what very well could be bodies in the road, and a second later a shudder shakes the whole vehicle. I squeeze my eyes shut, encasing myself in darkness while Jim presses me down harder, but it does nothing to block out the movement of the car or the terror swirling through me at the unknown.

I stay down until Jim's hand moves from my head, and then I'm up, looking out the window as we barrel down the road. There's a hole in the windshield and the glass has splintered into a spider web pattern that makes it hard to see the road in front of us. Gray smoke billows from the engine, and the bumping of the car as we roar down the street tells me the tires have been shot out.

On either side of us are fields, empty and free of people who want to capture and torture us, and I spin around to find the town fading in the distance. There's no one behind us either. At least not as far as I can tell.

"Are we safe?" I ask.

When I turn to face Jim, my heart almost stops beating. His face is contorted in pain, and he's gripping the steering wheel so tightly now that it looks like his hands have been welded to the plastic. The right sleeve of his shirt is dark red, the spot growing larger by the second.

"You're shot!"

I pull my seatbelt off and slide closer to him, getting up on my knees as he drives. His foot pushes the pedal against the floor, the needle edging close to seventy. His face is

182

clammy and his body shakes as he refuses to let go.

"Slow down!"

I scoot closer, scanning him so I can figure out where he's been shot. His arm is soaked to his elbow, the blood thick and dark on his bicep. I can't get to it while he's driving, though. It's on the other side of his body.

"We have to stop!"

He shakes his head and I swear we move faster. Everything we have is in the backseat, so I can't get to the first aid stuff at the moment. With as much as he's bleeding, though, he's liable to pass out at any second. Which is going to be bad for both of us since we're now moving close to eighty miles an hour.

I sit back long enough to pull my shirt over my head, then scoot closer to Jim, putting my body right against his so I can reach across him and press the shirt to the wound. I push hard and his whole body jerks, but he doesn't try to move my hand.

When I look back out the front window, the smoke coming from the engine has grown dark. Almost black. It billows out, making our visibility even more limited than it was a second ago.

We're going to wreck if he doesn't stop soon.

I cover his right hand with my free one, trying to give him a reassuring pat. "Slow down. We're okay."

His fingers relax, and I feel the car slow under me. I watch as the needle moves backwards, passing seventy, then sixty, moving down to fifty. When it's under forty, I turn to face Jim.

His eyes meet mine. *"Are you okay?"*

"I'm fine. You're the one we need to check out. You need to find a place to stop."

He nods as he turns his gaze back to the road. I focus on pressing my shirt more firmly against the gunshot wound.

How he can see I don't know, but after a few minutes the SUV slows even more. He turns into what looks like an overgrown driveway. Weeds and branches close in

183

around us the deeper he goes, finally pulling to a stop less than a minute later. Through the cracks in the windshield and the smoke pouring from the engine, the roof of a house is just visible. Good. It will give me a chance to take care of him.

He pulls the key out of the ignition, but the smoke doesn't stop. Shit. If those assholes are looking for us, they may be able to follow the trail of smoke. Hopefully, they'll decide we aren't worth the trouble.

When I turn to face Jim, I find his eyes closed and his expression pained. From this angle, I can't get a good look at his arm, so I move closer, practically climbing onto his lap. He lifts his head and opens his eyes a crack, but his lips don't move. Not that it matters. I'm too focused on his injury to have a conversation right now. With no medical training, I have to pray that not only did the bullet go straight through, but that it didn't hit anything major.

I move my shirt, now saturated with his blood, and tear his clothes away so I can examine the wound. Blood oozes from the injury, so thick it's hard to see. I do the only thing I can think to do: grab a bottle of water and pour it over his shoulder, washing the blood away until I can see it better.

"It went all the way through," I say, leaning closer so I can get a good look at it. "But I don't know how bad it is."

Jim's good hand grabs my chin, turning my face toward his. We're inches apart when his lips move. *"Let's get inside. We're too out in the open here."*

I nod as I slide off his lap.

We climb out of the car, me on my side and Jim on his. Branches scrape against my bare stomach and arms, leaving scratches behind as I head for the back door. I need a shirt and my rifle. After I get Jim settled, I can come back out for the medical supplies, food, and water.

I grab a shirt out of my bag and pull it over my head, then sling my carbine over my shoulder. When I reach the front of the SUV, I find Jim leaning against a tree, holding my shirt against his still-bleeding wound.

The smoke coming from the engine has slowed enough

that I feel confident no one would be able to follow it. We should be good here. At least until we can figure out what to do next.

I turn to face the house but stop dead in my tracks. It's more like a shack, probably not even livable twenty years ago. Every one of the windows is broken or cracked, and the front door is hanging open. Who knows what animals have made their homes in this place. Great. We'd be better off in the SUV, assuming we're sure it isn't going to burst into flames.

"You think this is safe?" I say when I turn to face Jim.

He shrugs, then winces. *"I don't know."*

Damn. He's hurting bad.

"Let me check it out." I ignore the way he lifts his eyebrows as I slip my rifle off my shoulder. "Stay here."

My back is to him already, so if he argues or tells me to be careful, I don't see it.

I head for the house, studying my surroundings as I go, my feet sinking into the soft earth. The roof is intact, which means we'd have cover, but nothing else about the house is very reassuring. It's going to be dirty — not exactly good news for an open wound — and probably crawling with creatures. I try not to let the shiver that runs down my spine shake my body. Jim's behind me, most likely watching every move I make, and the last thing I want him to know is that I'm worried or scared or unsure if we're going to make it out of this alive.

When I reach the front door, I pause and step to the left, knocking on the frame so anything lurking inside knows I'm here. I hold my breath while I wait to see what happens. When nothing comes running, I push the door open wider. It's stiff, like the hinges have been rusted through and aren't used to moving, but I manage to get it open wide enough to step inside. Just like I thought, the room is covered in webs and dirt, with long-dead leaves crowded in every corner. An old chair that looks like it went to a dining room table from the seventies leans against one wall, but otherwise the place is empty.

This isn't going to work.

I go back outside, my gaze sweeping across the clearing for any signs of trouble as I move. Jim is still leaning against the tree, his eyes closed despite the fact that he's out in the open and something could sneak up on him. He has the benefit of being able to hear.

Thankfully, the engine has stopped smoking completely now. We may not be in danger of the car bursting into flames.

"Jim," I say when I kneel in front of him.

One eye opens. *"We going in?"*

"It's no good. The car is better. Let me get you in the backseat so I can dress your wound."

He doesn't argue, and he lets me help him to his feet. Every move makes his expression even more pinched. My shirt is now so soaked with his blood that it's become useless. I'd toss it in the forest if I wasn't afraid it'd draw zombies our way. I have no idea if they can smell blood, but I'm not willing to take a chance.

I help Jim into the backseat and climb in after him. Once the door is shut, I flip on the overhead light. It's dim but provides enough illumination to allow me to see what I'm doing. Thank God Dad brought all that first aid stuff home at the beginning of the apocalypse.

I rip open a bottle of rubbing alcohol, pausing just before I pour it over the wound to say, "This is going to hurt."

Jim's whole body jerks, but he doesn't pull away. I soak the front of the wound, then the back, being sure to get a good amount inside. Then I pack it with sterile gauze and wrap a bandage around his arm. Within seconds, blood has begun to seep through the white gauze. We're just going to have to wait and pray that the bleeding slows.

When Jim leans his head back and closes his eyes, so do I.

We're alive, which is saying something, but the emotional damage that seeing Dad's car has left behind is threatening to crush me right now. I knew he was dead, but before I saw that car and that town and those men, I was able to imagine that he'd met a sudden end. Maybe shot in the back of the head by some asshole who wanted the supplies he'd gathered. That's the best case scenario in a world like this. Now, though, every time I close my eyes, I see that naked, decaying body hanging on the fence. Who knows what those men did to my dad before they killed him?

And now we're in deep shit. Jim's hurt and we are literally out in the middle of nowhere. Probably no more than thirty miles from my house, but too far away to walk back. And we're still close to two hundred and fifty miles away from Atlanta.

I'm not sure it could get much worse.

CHAPTER TWENTY-FIVE

JIM

The throbbing in my arm doesn't let up, and every time I move it pulses through my whole body. So I just lean my head against the seat with my eyes closed while the silence around us grows heavier.

It's the pain in my chest that seems to be the most crippling part of this situation, though. If Amira is blaming me for the shitty turn of events I don't want to know, so I keep my eyes squeezed shut while I silently berate myself. She trusted me and I promised I would do what I could to keep her safe. Less than ten minutes into the trip, and I proved what a major screw-up I really am. Driving into that town was a mistake, and not listening to my instincts may end up being the end for us.

Warm fingers touch my face, and I open my eyes to find Amira staring down at me. I was so lost in my thoughts that I didn't feel or hear her move. Maybe I fell asleep? I look around to discover that the forest surrounding us is darker now. It has to be late evening, meaning I was out for a while. Not good. I have to be more aware of my surroundings. I promised I'd be her ears.

"Are you hungry?" Amira's voice booms through the small space, and not for the first time, I find myself wishing I knew sign language. Not that it would matter right now. My left arm is pretty useless, thanks to the asshole who shot me.

"No." I force myself to sit up, sucking in a deep breath when pain pulses up and down my arm. It feels like I just got all my strength back after that damn cut on my leg, and here I am hurt again. Only now we don't have the safety of Amira's house.

She frowns, her brown eyes moving from my face to my arm. I follow her gaze to the red spot in the center of the gauze. It hasn't grown since the last time I looked at it, so the bleeding must have slowed.

"These should help with the pain," she says.

The two little white pills in her hand call out to me.

"Thanks."

I pop the pills in my mouth and wash them down with a gulp of water, thankful that her dad seemed to have a stash of every drug imaginable. The interior of the car has gotten toasty since we first climbed in the backseat, and the longer we sit here, the worse it's going to get. Not like we have another option. I pulled off here because there didn't seem to be another damn place to stop at as far as the eye could see. If we'd gone much farther, the engine would have overheated for sure. Which means we're going to have to walk if we want to get out of here. Not exactly ideal, thanks to the fact that I'm hurt—again.

"Are you usually this injury prone, or is it the apocalypse that brings it out in you?" Amira asks after a few seconds of silence.

So I'm not the only one thinking about my last injury. She's probably realizing what a pain in the ass I am. Since we met, she's had to exert a lot of energy to keep me alive, and I can't help wondering if she's starting to think I'm not worth it.

"I'm sorry," I say, focusing on her face so she'll be able to read my lips. "I wanted to take care of you."

She frowns when she shakes her head. "I don't need anyone to take care of me."

"I know." This isn't coming out the way I wanted it to. "I know you can take care of yourself. Better than most people can. But I *wanted* to take care of you."

Amira's frown deepens and she shakes her head like she doesn't have the first clue what I'm saying. Maybe I'm delirious. Maybe this time the fever will sweep me away and drag me down to hell where I belong.

"Never mind." I close my eyes and lean back against the seat. "I was never good for anything before the zombies came, so I don't know why it surprises me that nothing has changed."

"Open your eyes." Amira's voice booms through the small space.

My heart jumps to my throat, and I sit up so fast that pain pulses up and down my arm. But I force myself to stay upright as I look out the window, expecting zombies or men to be surrounding the car. The dark forest is just as clear as it was a second ago, though, and everything is quiet. Still.

When I turn, I come face to face with Amira's intense glare. "What does that mean?"

"What?" My mind spins, trying to figure out what she's so pissed about, but I come up empty.

"That you were never good for anything?" she says, her voice becoming louder in the small space. "You told me this was your chance to start over. You sacrificed your life to save your friends. You saved me when those men came to the house."

"What the hell does that have to do with dragging you out to the middle of nowhere just so we can die in this car?" I raise my voice even though I know it's wasted effort. She can't hear me, so yelling at her isn't going to get my

191

point across any more than whispering the damn words would, but it makes me feel better. At least a little.

"We are not going to die in this car." Amira grabs my chin, and her fingers dig into my flesh like she's trying to crush me. "And you are not useless. You saved me from dying in that house because that's what I would have done if you hadn't come along. I would have hidden in there for the rest of my life and died alone just so I didn't have to face the fact that my dad wasn't coming back. You made me choose life."

"A lot of good it did you. You'd be better off if I'd died in a field somewhere and never made it to your house."

Amira's mouth scrunches up as she studies me. "I'm glad you found me. I'm glad I met you."

"This whole thing is strange for me," I say, shaking my head. "Feeling like someone else's life is more important than my own."

She frowns, studying me for a second before saying, "Didn't you feel that way about your wife? You married her, you must have loved her."

"I thought I did." Thinking about me and Becky, and how things were between us before we got married versus how they were at the end. It's hard to reconcile the two. It doesn't seem like the same couple. "When it ended, though, there wasn't much left between us but bitterness. And it was never like this."

That's an understatement. The pang inside me when I think about losing Amira is like nothing I ever felt with Becky. Maybe I never loved my wife. Not really. Does that mean I love Amira, though?

Her eyes are still on me like she's trying to work out the words I just said and what they mean, and it hits me that she's picking up the same thing. That I might be in love with her.

Before I even have a chance to decide what to say next, she kisses me.

CHAPTER TWENTY-SIX

AMIRA

I don't know what I'm thinking when I press my lips to his, but I know it feels right. When his mouth moves against mine, when his good hand slides up my back, when he pulls me over so I'm straddling him. It's like I was always meant to be here with Jim. In his arms.

Even if we die in this SUV, it will all have been worth it.

Jim pulls back, his blue eyes searching mine. His hand still on my back. *"We should be more careful."*

"Being careful would mean I'd still be cowering in that attic, and I don't want to be that person," I say. "You found my house for a reason, and we both know the end could come at any second. We've both been afraid of how this thing between us might complicate life, which is dumb. And I'm done being dumb. I don't want either one of us to die with regrets."

Jim only holds my gaze for a second longer before pulling me back to him. His lips slide over mine, then down my neck to my chest.

I run my fingers through his hair, gripping the back of his neck as his lips move over the tops of my breasts. His good hand slides up my side, stopping just under my bra. Then his mouth is back on mine. Kissing me as if a horde is closing in on us and we only have seconds left. Every move he makes feels desperate, like he wants to take in as much of me as he can.

We kiss until Jim pulls back, and when I open my eyes, his expression is pained. Damn that gunshot wound. All those nights he lay next to me, his body heat seeping into me. Calling out to me. And I didn't take advantage of the roof we had over our heads. It was stupid and a total waste.

"We can stop," I say, trying to slide off his lap.

Jim's good hand grabs my waist. *"Don't go anywhere."*

"You're hurting."

"I don't want you to move."

His hand goes up my back and he pulls me against him. I rest my head on his good shoulder, closing my eyes. His heart thumps against my chest, matching the rhythm of my own.

He's hurting and I know he needs rest, but I can't bring myself to leave this position.

JIM IS OUT COLD AND THE SUV IS PITCH BLACK, BUT I can't sleep. Every shadow that moves across the forest makes my heart pound harder. There could be a million threatening things surrounding us right now, but I'd never hear the sounds warning us that they're coming. Bombs could be going off somewhere, and I wouldn't have a clue until one dropped on our heads.

I know Jim needs time to heal, but I'm not sure how long I'll be able to stay here. Trapped in this car where the air gets thicker and more humid by the second. Knowing there's no way to escape if those assholes do manage to find us. It has

194

me feeling more claustrophobic than the attic ever did.

We have to move. Tomorrow.

I shift so I'm facing the back of the SUV, my gaze moving over the supplies we brought from the house as I take a mental inventory. Extra clothes, food, weapons, and water. There's so much the space is practically bursting at the seams. We can't take it all with us, though, not traveling on foot. We won't even be able to take a quarter of it. Just the essentials.

There's nothing scarier than the realization that you're about to cross hundreds of miles of zombie-infested country with little to no supplies.

I glance Jim's way to make sure he's still out before turning to face the back, making a mental checklist of what we absolutely have to take. A gun each, as well as a knife or two, and enough water for one day. Some food, but not a lot—we can find more on the road if we need to. First aid supplies and any medicine we have with us. Basically, whatever we take will have to fit in one backpack each. Carrying too much will slow us down.

The picture of my family is the only other thing I can't do without. Everything else I can leave. So what if I have to wear the same clothes for a couple days? I can hack it. But I can't walk away from that picture. It could be the last time I ever get to see their faces.

I dig through the back until I find it, trying my best to keep my movements slow and quiet. But it's impossible to know how much sound I make when I pop the back off the frame and slide the picture out.

The photo is eight by ten inches, which means I'll have to fold it in half if I want it to fit easily in my backpack. I take my time making the creases, putting them where they will do the least amount of damage. The last thing I want to do is to ruin the smiling faces on the paper.

When I turn back, I find Jim awake and watching me, his blue eyes sparkling in the darkness of the car. *"What are you doing?"*

"I'm sorry," I say as I slip the picture into the front pocket of my backpack. "I didn't mean to wake you."

Jim shifts, only wincing a little as he turns his body to face me. *"It's okay."*

"We can't stay here." Long shadows are visible through the window at his back, and the way they move makes them seem alive and malicious. "We have to keep moving."

Jim's hand slides up my leg to my thigh, and he gives it a gentle squeeze. *"I know."*

"You'll be able to do it? I think we should leave at dawn."

"I'll be okay. We just have to make it far enough on foot to find a car. Right?"

"I don't want to push you, but being out here makes me uneasy. We're too close to that town still. Anything could sneak up on us."

"Don't worry about me. I just want to get you somewhere safe."

I swallow down my words: is there a safe place out there? He claims there is, but we have no way of knowing until we actually make it to Atlanta.

"Okay. Then you should get some rest. I'll keep watch."

He nods even though the expression on his face says he wants to argue. Of course, right now there's no way he'd win. We have to start walking tomorrow. I can power through, but he's been shot. He needs to take it easy. Gather all the strength he can to make it through the trip. Who knows if or when we'll be able to find a car.

He shifts on the other side of the seat, settling in as best as he can with his injured arm probably throbbing like crazy. It's too early to give him another pill, plus I don't want to run out too soon. I only have four left, and Jim may need the help tomorrow.

The rise and fall of Jim's chest slows, and when I'm sure he's out, I let my mind wander. It's scary, thinking about all the things that can go wrong, but it makes me feel more prepared to know what I could be facing. Even if I know I'm only fooling myself.

196

I'm not sure exactly when zombies became the least of my concerns, but somewhere over the last few months, they did. They are a very real and present threat, no one can deny that, but there are so many other things that can go wrong. At least the zombies are predictable. Men aren't. We don't know who we can and can't trust, or where they might be lurking. The same goes for Atlanta. Jim heard it was safe, but he has no real proof of that. We could make it all the way there, across three hundred miles of hostile country, just to discover that what lies in store for us within the walls of Atlanta is worse than anything we could have faced out here.

It's a terrifying reality to be confronted with.

The longer I sit in the silence, the more my mind goes back to what happened today. I've tried to put it aside, to think of something else, but I can't. Dad is dead. I knew it, but seeing the proof in the face of everything else we've gone through sends an ache pulsing through me. Whatever he went through in that town, I hope it was quick. That they didn't make him suffer.

Images that are too horrifying to be real flip through my head, and I try to brush them away. It's impossible, though. Sitting in the silence of the car with the darkness surrounding us, I can't think of anything else. Even if I could sleep right now, I wouldn't want to. I can't imagine the nightmares I'd have.

I'm still wide awake when the darkness starts to lift. Before long, Jim stirs, and when a warm hand covers mine, I allow my eyes to close. If he weren't with me, I'm not sure I'd be able to face today. Not after all the horrors I imagined are waiting for us.

Jim gives my hand a squeeze, and I open my eyes as I turn to face him. *"You want to get a little sleep before we head out?"*

"I'm fine." I slip my hand out of his and grab my pack off the floor. "I'd rather get moving. The sooner we can put some more distance between us and that town, the better."

197

Jim frowns, but I'm not sure if his concern is for me or for his ability to get through the day. Doesn't matter, though. We're both going to have to put our wounds aside if we want to survive.

"Let's get you a pain pill before we head out."

I'm digging through my bag when Jim grabs my chin and turns my face toward his. His touch is gentle and warm. Comforting. His gaze holds mine, and it too is soft.

"I'm sorry about your dad. I wanted to talk to you about it last night, but I wasn't sure if you needed time to absorb it."

"I knew he was dead," I say, swallowing around the lump of tears rising in my throat. Trying to force their way out. "At least now I have closure."

I'm not sure what my voice sounds like to Jim, if he can hear the emotion-choked lie in my words or not, but I know that the tears in my eyes give me away for sure. I blink, trying to get them to go away before we both drown, but it doesn't work. They fall from my eyes and slide down my cheeks, scorching me with their heat. It's like lava on my skin.

Jim wraps his arms around me, pulling me against him and crushing my bag between us. The pill bottle I was looking for rests in the palm of my hand, and when the sobs break out of me, my fingers wrap around it so tightly that they nearly crush the plastic. I cry, and my whole body shakes as emotions I've been trying to hide for weeks burst out of me. I have no family left. The girl I was a year ago is gone, and so is the world of hope and promise that she lived in. My life wasn't perfect and there were a lot of times when I felt like an alien in this world of music and laughter and sounds I couldn't enjoy, but at least I knew I would be able to find my way. Now, in this new world of death and violence, I'm not sure it's possible to create anything good.

Jim pulls back a little, barely loosening his grip on me, and his lips brush against my cheek as he kisses the tears away. His arm has to be killing him, but even when I try to wiggle from his grasp, he doesn't let me go. It's like he wants to hold on to me for the rest of his life.

"I don't want to hurt you," I say, finally twisting my body enough to break free.

I swipe the back of my hand across my cheeks, the pill bottle still pressed against my palm as I erase the last evidence of my weakness from sight.

"It's okay. Don't worry about me."

"Of course I'm going to worry about you." I pop the bottle open and hand him one of the little white pills. "You were shot less than a day ago."

"It's not that bad."

When I roll my eyes, the last of the moisture hiding in them threatens to spill out. I turn away from Jim so I can wipe it away while gathering the things I want to take. "We should get moving while the sun is still low."

Jim doesn't force me to turn so he can answer, and I look back to find him getting his own stuff together.

It doesn't take long for us to be ready, and when we head out, the sun is still low and the forest is cloaked in shadows. With Jim at my side, it's less threatening than it was last night, but not much.

Every step he takes seems to hurt him. With one arm injured, he carries both his pack and the AK-47 on the same shoulder, and by the time we make it out of the woods and onto the main road, sweat has beaded on his forehead. It's late June and hot despite the fact that the sun isn't up yet, but we both know it's only going to get worse as the day goes on.

We have to find a car or I don't know if we'll make it.

Jim pushes himself harder than anyone I've ever seen, and before I know it, we've been on the road for hours. The sun is high above us—and more unforgiving than a nun in Catholic school—and we are both drenched in sweat. We pass a water bottle back and forth, taking small sips in hopes of conserving what little bit of water we have.

As the day wears on, Jim's expression becomes more and more pinched, and before long I start to worry that he's going to fall over. Every step seems to take him more effort.

"Just a little longer," I say as I take the water from him. "Then we'll find a car. You just have to hang in there for a little bit longer."

He nods even though we both know the words could be a lie.

CHAPTER TWENTY-SEVEN

JIM

I push myself. One foot in front of the other, ignoring the constant throb in my arm and the sun scorching down on me from above. Amira walks at my side, so close her arm brushes mine every few steps. She never slows. Never seems to tire. Even as the sun gets higher and the water we carry with us gets warmer, her pace stays consistent.

It helps keep me going, too.

Her stamina is amazing, but it can't last forever. No matter how determined she is, eventually she'll run out of steam. With over two hundred miles to go, we have no choice but to find a car. Walking like this will take forever and leaves us exposed to any number of dangers. Plus, the longer we walk, the more my legs start to feel like half-cooked spaghetti noodles.

It's late afternoon before I spot a good place, and by then every inch of me has started to tremble. I grab Amira's hand as I come to a stop, breathing so heavily that at first I can't talk. My body is drenched in sweat, and my shirt sticks to my back like it's a second set of skin.

Amira looks up at me expectantly, but even after I've caught my breath, I'm too focused on our surroundings to say anything. In the distance, a few houses are visible on the other side of a weed-choked field. If we head that way, we can not only rest for the night, but possibly find a vehicle.

"There —" I point even though I know she has to focus on my lips to catch what I'm saying, and I don't miss the way my hand trembles from the exhaustion pulsing through me. " — we should head that way. Maybe that house will have a car."

When she's sure I'm done talking, she turns toward the field, scanning the area slowly before nodding. "Okay."

I grab her shoulder so I can turn her back to face me. "We can sleep there tonight if nothing else."

She nods again, her eyes sweeping over my face like she can see inside me. Thanks to the sun, a splash of red now coats her cheeks and nose under her dark skin. Next to her I look like an albino lobster. Sunburn wasn't even something I'd considered when we set out this morning, but standing under the rays, it hits me what a big threat something as simple as the sun is these days. Shit. I get so worried about zoms and men who want nothing more than to exploit everyone they come across that I forget the little things.

"How are you?" she asks when neither one of us talks.

"Exhausted." I drop my hand from her shoulder and look toward the waiting house, keeping my face pointed her way. "Let's get there so I can rest."

I don't say that I'm not sure how much longer my legs will be able to hold me up, but I know I don't need to. She isn't dumb, and she's more observant than the average person. There's no way she missed the tremors that are now moving through my body.

Amira slips the carbine off her shoulder. My arm aches so much that waves of pain move through me, but it goes through my mind that we'll have a roof over our heads and

202

possibly a bed. It's not what I should be focusing on right now, but I can't help it. This girl is unlike anyone I've ever known, and I can't stand the idea of not having my hands on her. Every second of every day, I want her with me. Next to me. The idea of letting her out of my sight hurts more than the gunshot wound.

"Let's go." Her voice echoes across the emptiness.

I slide my right hand down her arm and lace my fingers with hers and start walking. It's a good mile—at least—and we keep our pace even and steady. Not slow, but not in such a hurry that we're liable to miss anything.

My eyes don't stop moving. Going from the house to the area past it, studying both sides and even behind us. Then to Amira. Taking in her profile and her expression as she, too, keeps an eye on our surroundings. The look on her face is so severe. Deadly serious. Like she could kill anything that crossed her path with her bare hands. I believe it, too. She's that strong.

A slow chime rings through the air when we're still a good distance off, making me stop in my tracks. Amira, who can't hear it, gives me a questioning look.

I nod toward the house. "I hear something."

Her eyebrows shoot up and her hand tightens on the rifle. "People? A zombie?"

I shake my head while I scan the distance. Looking for anything that might be moving. "Maybe a wind chime?"

"Should we wait?"

I pause for a second, listening to the chime as I watch the trees sway. Maybe I'm imagining it, but it seems like the two match.

A wave of dizziness sweeps over me and I close my eyes, tightening my grip on Amira's hand. My knees almost buckle, but I fight against it. Force them to stay firm.

We don't have much of a choice right now, so I open my eyes and start walking again, pulling Amira with me. "Let's go."

We reach the yard and the house comes into better view, but the massive yard still stretches out in front of us. So wide and open that it makes my legs tremble again. The throbbing in my arm has increased by leaps and bounds, and we still have a good distance to go.

I pause, trying to make it seem like I'm looking everything over, not trying to gather my strength, but the look Amira gives me says that she knows I'm full of shit. We still have to pass the barn, as well as a couple smaller sheds, but from where we are the house looks deserted. The door is hanging open and the yard overrun with weeds. The collection of leaves gathered on the porch seems to be undisturbed. The only sounds other than the wind chime are the chatter of birds and the sway of the trees above our heads. It's as silent as the rest of the world has been.

I force my legs to move, focusing on Amira's hand in mine. Trying to absorb some of her strength. As we approach the porch, I let her hand go and slide the rifle off my good shoulder. My entire body may be weak and shaky, but I refuse to go in unprepared.

Amira raises the carbine as we head up the steps. I go first, but with my arm, I'm weaker than a damn kitten. Hopefully, adrenaline gets me through any confrontation that comes my way.

I kick the door open with the toe of my boot, my heart jumping when the creak of its hinges echoes through the house. Amira steps in front of me, putting herself between me and the open door.

"Stop—" I reach for her arm, but I'm forced to slump against the wall when the world sways. If the house wasn't behind me, I'd be on my ass for sure.

Amira doesn't even glance my way before stepping inside. Her back is stiff as she moves forward, the rifle ready and her eyes scanning the room. From where I'm sitting, I can't see that far into the house, and in seconds she's disappeared from sight. I listen to the sound of her feet scraping against the floor and the creak of the wood as she moves, echoing so loudly that it has the hair on my neck standing on end. She has no clue how much noise she makes in this world, and it's terrifying.

"Shit." I try to push myself up, but my head is too light, and all I end up doing is crashing back down. "Who's making all the noise now," I mutter.

Feet scuffle across the floor, the rhythm different than the small steps Amira has been taking, and fear clenches my gut. A grunt follows only a second later, and I'm moving forward. Pulling myself through the house on my stomach, my injury throbbing with every move I make. The AK-47, hooked over my good arm, scrapes against the floor and sweat has beaded on my face, but I don't slow.

I make it through the living room as the sounds of a struggle increase, and when I turn the corner, I nearly collide with the putrid face of a zombie. His lifeless, milky eyes stare at me from where he lies, flat on his back just inside the doorway. A knife sticks out of his head and black goo puddles under his skull, filling the room with its stench.

Another grunt draws my attention across the room to where Amira struggles with a second zombie. This one smaller, a girl who probably wasn't more than sixteen when she died. Still, she is almost a head taller than Amira and seems to have the upper hand. The two girls struggle, the dead one snapping her teeth as Amira tries to push her back against the wall. She doesn't seem to be making much progress. Plus, her knife is in the other zombie's head and the carbine is lying on the floor a few feet behind her.

"I got you," I say even though I know she can't hear me.

I drag myself to my feet, gritting my teeth against the pain radiating through my arm. When I have a good position—and I'm sure I'm not going to pass out—I pull the AK-47 from my shoulder and take aim. Or try to, anyway. My arms are shaking so badly that I can't get the zombie girl in my sights. She and Amira are moving too much, and the throb in my arm isn't helping. If I pull the trigger now, I may end up shooting the wrong person.

"Shit," I mutter as I toss the gun aside and push myself up off the ground.

Everything sways as I pull my knife, but I make my legs move anyway. One foot forward, then the other. Darkness closes in from both sides, but I blink and force it back.

"Here!" I call as I charge across the room. "Look at me!"

I wave the knife toward the zombie as if the blade will magically lodge itself in her brain. My vision is so blurry that when she turns my way, at first I'm pretty sure I imagined it. When the snarl she lets out radiates through me, I know I haven't.

"That's right. Keep walking."

"Jim!" Amira's voice echoes through the room, seeming to come from miles away.

I turn toward the sound, my brain fuzzy and unfocused, and shake my head. It only makes my body sway and the room tip at an awkward angle.

What was I doing?

My fingers tighten around something hard, and I look down to find the knife in my hand.

The zombie girl.

When I look back, she's almost on top of me. Her brown teeth are bared like she's a rabid dog, and her black fingers are so close that I can see the dried blood under her nails.

I stumble back but only make it one step before the crack of a gunshot echoes through the air. The girl's head jerks to the side and black blood sprays everywhere, and then she's down. I'm not far behind, my body falling so fast it's like I've been shot as well. When I hit the wood floor, pain spreads through my arm and nearly blinds me.

"Jim!"

Darkness rolls across my vision, blocking out everything. I can still hear Amira's voice as she asks me if I'm okay, but I can't see a damn thing.

I reach up, and my fingers make contact with her smooth cheek.

Shit. Wouldn't it be a kick in the crotch if I end up blind?

206

CHAPTER TWENTY-EIGHT

AMIRA

My heart nearly explodes when Jim hits the floor.

I'm not sure if I scream his name or just think it, but I know that when I fall to my knees at his side it's so hard it radiates through me, shaking my teeth to the roots. His eyes roll back until there is nothing but whites, but his lips are still moving when his hand reaches up to brush my cheek.

...blind. Then we'd be fucked.

I don't even have time to let his words sink in before his eyes close and his hand drops to the ground.

"Jim." I shake his shoulders, but he doesn't move, so I press my face against his chest and hold my breath. Waiting for his heart to thump against my cheek. It only takes a second. Thank God.

When I'm sure he's not dead, I sit back and let out a deep sigh while I look the place over. The two zombies I killed—a father and daughter—have filled the room with a stench that makes my eyes water, and even though nothing else has come running, I know I need to search the house and make sure it's clear.

I leave Jim where he is and head back to the front door, the carbine draped over my shoulder. Once the door is locked, I take my time searching the house. Room by room, keeping my back to the wall and my eyes open for any signs of movement. Just like I thought, though, the two zombies I already killed are the only ones in the house.

When I'm sure the place is clear, I head back down to check on Jim. Even from the doorway I can see the rise and fall of his chest, which is a huge relief. Hopefully, he just needs some rest. It's been a long day, and between the walking, the sun, the lack of food, and the possibility that he could be a little dehydrated, it's no wonder his injury knocked him on his ass.

I need to check the garage, get these bodies out of here, and then check on Jim's wound.

In that order?

I give Jim a good once-over and decide to deal with his injury first. If he gets another infection, we could be in real trouble.

I hold my breath as I run my hand across his forehead. His skin is damp and warm, but not hot. Not boiling the way it was when I first found him.

When I peel the gauze from his wound, I'm even more relieved. It hasn't started bleeding again, and there's nothing about it that looks alarming. No red streaks or red, shiny skin. It just looks like a gunshot wound, which is something I never thought I'd be happy to see.

Once I have the wound cleaned and redressed, I turn my focus on the zombies.

The man is bigger, so I deal with him first, wanting to get the hard part over with as fast as possible. I find a blanket on the couch and wrap it around his head so I don't leave a trail behind, then grab hold of his legs and pull. It takes a lot of effort to get him out of the room, and by the time I have him out the front door, I'm dripping with sweat.

I'm gasping for breath as I head back, grabbing a blanket on the way so I can once again absorb the black goo seeping from the dead zombie. The girl probably weighs less than I do, but I'm so worn out from my day of walking that it seems to take me twice as much effort to get her out onto the porch. By the time I'm back inside and have the door relocked, all I want to do is curl up on a couch and sleep.

But I still need to look for a car.

In the kitchen, I find four hooks mounted on the wall next to what I'm assuming is the door into the garage. Only two have keys dangling from them. The first set has a John Deere key chain, so I leave those where they are and slip the others off their hook. Hanging from a key ring shaped like Florida, the words *I love Panama City* printed across the state, are two keys and a keyless entry fob. The little buttons that indicate lock and unlock aren't what draw my attention, though, it's the third one. The one that tells me this car has a remote starter.

When I shove the garage door open, it's so dark that I can't see a hand in front of my face. I inhale slowly, trying to ignore the stench the zombies I dragged outside left behind in my nostrils, focusing on the room in front of me. Nothing is moving as far as I can tell, and there doesn't seem to be any rot clinging to the air, so I push the button on the key fob. In front of me, the headlights on a red Dodge Ram 4x4 flip on. Perfect for running zombies over—assuming it has enough gas to get us to Atlanta.

I open the driver's side door and pull myself in, nearly collapsing in relief when I get a look at the gas gauge. More than half a tank. Hopefully, that's enough.

Now that I'm behind the wheel of a car and we have a roof over our heads for the next few hours, I allow my body to relax. My shoulders slump and I lay my head down, resting it on the steering wheel right between my hands. I've done everything I could to be strong today, knowing how tough the journey was for Jim and how much strength it took just to put one foot in front of the other. Now, though, I feel drained. Like someone cut me open and dumped out all my insides. Thank God we don't have to walk tomorrow, because I don't think I could.

After a few seconds, I turn the truck off and head back into the house. I'm exhausted and have little energy left to do anything, but I need to check on Jim. Maybe even try to get him awake enough to coax him into a bed. Or at the very least, a couch. With a little luck, we'll both be rested enough to move on tomorrow.

CHAPTER TWENTY-NINE

JIM

My back throbs when I come to, and even before I'm totally conscious, I know it doesn't have anything to do with my gunshot. I shift, rolling to my side, and the hard wood floor digs into my arm. The groan I let out is so loud it could probably wake the dead.

The dead. Shit.

My eyes fly open, and I look around. The room around me is lit up, but the light coming in from the windows is soft. Early morning or late evening, it's hard to tell. I'm still on the floor, but the zombie Amira was fighting when I passed out is nowhere in sight, and neither is the other one. I can barely remember what happened. Did she take care of the girl? She must have, or the creature would have chewed on me while I slept. With as exhausted as I was, I doubt I would have felt it.

Not only are the zombies gone, but the floor has been cleaned up, which means the room doesn't reek the way it did. It's still hotter than hell, though. And stuffy. Like the windows haven't been opened in months. My entire body is drenched in sweat, and every inch of me is sore too. Now I know why, though. I'm still on the hard wood floor where I passed out.

"Amira." I mumble her name because I know she can't hear me, but it only takes me a second to find her.

Asleep on a couch on the other side of the room, she has the carbine propped up next to her. With the way her hand is resting on it, I get the impression she fell asleep trying to keep watch. It's no wonder. She didn't sleep last night either, and we walked all day.

I manage to make it to my feet somehow and cross the room to her. By the time I get there my legs feel like they each weigh a hundred pounds. I drop to the floor next to her, gently moving the rifle so she doesn't freak out and try to kill me, and then shake her shoulders.

Her eyes fly open and she's up in a second, her hands reaching for the rifle just like I knew they would.

"It's okay."

I put my hand on Amira's knee, and when her brown eyes land on me, she lets out a sigh that's so full of relief it sends a pang through me. This girl could win an Academy Award. That's how good she is at acting like everything is fine. With as cool and determined as she was during that whole day of walking, I didn't have a damn clue that she was this worried. But I can see it now. Even with the grogginess still in her eyes, the relief is written in every line of her body.

"You're okay?" She slides down until she's sitting next to me.

"I think I am." My arm throbs and my legs are still weak, but I don't feel the way I did the day I dragged myself into Amira's garage. Just exhausted. Hopefully, it won't matter how tired I am tomorrow, because I'll be behind the wheel of a car. "Did you check out the garage?"

"A truck. Half a tank." She gives me a shaky smile as she rests her hand on my knee. "You had me worried."

"Don't be." I lay my hand on top of hers. "I don't plan on leaving you alone any time soon."

Something flashes in her eyes, and her smile spreads until it's lighting up every inch of her face. "I'm going to hold you to that."

"Good."

Amira exhales again before saying, "Now that you're awake, I should check your wound again."

"Again?"

"I did it a few hours ago, when we first got here."

I glance toward the window as she starts to unwrap my arm. The sunlight shining through the window is a little more faded now, meaning it's evening. We still have hours ahead of us to rest up. Which we may need.

Amira leans closer to me, and I turn back to find her smile gone and her gaze focused on my arm as she unwraps the bandage. It stings, but with her so close to me, the pain barely registers. Suddenly, the fuzziness in my brain has nothing to do with the exhaustion or my sore body. In fact, I barely feel anything other than Amira's warm hands as they move up my arm. She scoots closer, most likely trying to get a better view of my injury, and I can't stop myself from running my good hand up her thigh.

She swats at me with her free hand. "Behave. You're injured and you need rest."

"I don't feel hurt. Not when you're this close to me."

She lifts her eyebrows as her gaze sweeps over me, taking in my expression. "We should wait. Get a little rest before we have to head out tomorrow."

"I've never been good at waiting."

"Well, you're going to have to learn. If we don't get this cleaned up, you could get another infection, and we don't have enough antibiotics to take care of it this time." Her smile falters but doesn't disappear completely. "If I lost you now, I'm not sure what I'd do with myself."

"You'd survive." I put my hand on her cheek, and she leans into it. "You are stronger than anyone I've ever known."

"You make me a stronger person."

Even though she's in the middle of dressing my wound, I pull her closer, crushing my lips against hers. She doesn't resist, but the kiss is still brief. I refuse to let her go completely, though, even after she's pulled away and she's gone back to bandaging my arm. I keep my good hand on her waist, right above the curve of her hip.

"If we make it to Atlanta," I say when she's done, "I don't plan on leaving the bedroom for at least a week."

"Not if." Amira's smile stretches wider than ever. "When. For now, though, we should get some rest."

She gets up, pulling me with her. My legs are still heavy as we head to the stairs, but I can't tear my gaze away from the sway of her hips. Not with the throbbing in my arm and the clouds clogging my brain.

Soon enough, we'll be in Atlanta, and then I'll make good on every promise I've made to her. Including the one about not leaving the bedroom for a week.

THE NEXT MORNING I FEEL LIKE A NEW MAN, EVEN IF that man isn't me. My body is sore from head to toe, but my legs don't threaten to give out when I stand and I still don't have a fever. With everything else going on, that's the best I can hope for.

Amira and I are anxious to reach our destination, so before the sun is barely over the horizon, we're on the road. The outside world flies by as I drive, passing empty fields and burned-out towns. Abandoned houses and businesses.

Even the silence in the car can't match the stillness of the world we now find ourselves in.

The lower the gas gauge dips, the more uneasiness settles in my gut. Even before the gas light comes on, I know we're not going to make it all the way, but I keep my worries to myself. No sense putting anything else on Amira's shoulders than what she's already had to take on.

The city comes into view, the buildings jutting into the blue sky and cutting across the horizon. From a distance, it's almost possible to convince myself everything is normal. There are no zombies, and the population of Atlanta is carrying on as usual. Going to work and school, paying bills and bitching about silly things like poor Wi-Fi and how their favorite show is once again a rerun.

The fantasy doesn't last long, though. The closer we get, the more the buildings come into focus, allowing me to appreciate the full damage the apocalypse has done to the city. There are holes in the skyline that were probably once occupied by skyscrapers, and a few other buildings have been cut in half, their tops jagged as if blown away.

"Were they bombed?" Amira asks, scooting to the edge of her seat so she can get a better view.

I shrug, wringing my hands on the steering wheel as I glance down at the gas gauge. The needle is so low I wouldn't be surprised if it broke off, but I still haven't mentioned to Amira that we're almost out of gas. I've been hoping I was somehow wrong and we'd make it all the way there. But now, as the wall comes into view, still so far in the distance that it feels like a tease, I know it isn't going to happen. We can go a mile or two more at most.

Amira turns to face me, her eyes on my lips. "What's wrong?"

"We're almost out of gas."

Her eyebrows shoot up. "Why didn't you tell me?"

"I was hoping we'd make it."

She shakes her head. "You can trust me not to overreact. You know that, right?"

"Yeah."

How can I explain that I don't want her to have to worry about anything ever again? I can't, because it's a feeling I still don't understand myself. I'm not used to it because other than Rachel, I've never had anyone I've wanted to keep safe like this before. Even when I ran out of that farmhouse to save Megan, it was more out of obligation to Jon, even if I didn't realize it at the time. With Amira, though, I would throw myself on a grenade and die with a smile on my face if it meant saving her from getting even a scratch.

She's still staring at me when the engine sputters and cuts out, and the truck drifts to a stop in the middle of the road. The freeway stretches out in front of us, and I can't stop staring at that wall. So close, yet so far.

I slam my hand into the steering wheel and let out a string of curse words so colorful I'm surprised a rainbow doesn't fly out of my mouth.

Amira puts her hand on my arm, which is so tight thanks to the grip I have on the steering wheel that I probably feel like a statue to her.

"Stop." Her voice is softer than usual. Calm. "We're going to be okay. We can do it."

I wish I had her confidence.

"You're right," I say, forcing my fingers to uncurl.

I turn, and she scoots closer, practically crawling over the center console and into my lap. When her lips brush against mine, they're soft and warm and welcoming. The kiss should calm me. Should help me relax, but for some reason it has the opposite affect. Tension rolls through my body, coiling around all the muscles in my arms and legs until they're tighter than ever before. The fear that comes with it is enough to make me feel like I'm on the verge of exploding. Knowing that we're about to go out there and face a city full of zombies. It's like my worst nightmare come true, especially with Amira at my side.

I can't let anything happen to her.

She pulls back and gives me a smile that doesn't reach her eyes. "Let's get our stuff together and go. No sense putting it off."

We gather everything we can comfortably carry and climb out. I grab the AK-47 and the little bit of ammo I have left, as well as my backpack. Amira has the carbine and her own pack, which is so stuffed with supplies I half expect her to fall over. She huffs when she pulls it on, but doesn't flinch or act like it's any heavier than a feather. If it starts to slow her down I'll say something, but until then, I let it go. She knows what she can and can't handle.

"Ready?" she says when she turns to face me.

Her voice echoes through the empty streets of Atlanta, carrying a hell of a lot further than it should.

"Maybe we should try to use hand signals as much as possible." I say, glancing around but keeping my face still so she can read my lips. "We don't know what's lurking around the next corner."

Her mouth turns down, and I let out a sigh of relief when she nods instead of answering. Thankfully, she isn't one of those overly sensitive women who gets furious when you point out something they've done wrong.

We head out, walking side by side as the hot sun shines down on us from above. Amira keeps her eyes moving, searching the empty spaces between the abandoned cars we pass as we head for the exit. Our pace is steady, and the quiet echo of our footsteps seems to be the only sound in the city at the moment. It's enough to make the hair on the back of my neck stand up.

The wind blows, and Amira's steps falter for the first time. When the scent of death hits me, I grab her hand and move faster. We're about to head deep into the city, and we both know what we're going to find. The stink of rot doesn't necessarily mean zombies are nearby. Not when hundreds of thousands of people used to live and work in this area.

"Keep moving," I say just in case she's looking my way.

Out of the corner of my eye, I see her head bob, but I don't slow enough to look her way. We reach the exit ramp without incident, only to discover that cement barriers have been placed across the road. Looks like we would have had to ditch the truck anyway.

"Shouldn't be far," I say, pulling Amira around the barriers and heading up the exit ramp and deeper into Atlanta.

When we reach the top, I freeze. The wall looms in front of us, bigger and more impressive now that we're closer, but still at least a mile off. Between safety and us sits street after street of the unknown. The buildings block out the sun, casting shadows across the street that send a shiver down my spine, and every breeze that comes our way is cloaked in death. It's faint, but present enough to have me on edge.

Next to me, Amira shivers as her eyes dart around. They're twice their normal size and so full of terror that I have the urge to drag her back to the truck and hide inside for the rest of our lives. Not that it would save us, but it would protect her from the current danger.

Instead, I give her hand a squeeze and start walking. After a couple steps, I let her go so I can pull the AK-47 off my shoulder, and she follows suit with her rifle. My palm is sweaty against the cool metal of the barrel, but the smooth wood of the rifle is soothing in my other hand.

We turn a corner, me less than two steps ahead of Amira, and I freeze at the sight of the horde blocking our way. There have to be more than a dozen of them dragging their feet against the road in front of us, filling the silent city with the scraping sound of soles on asphalt. Thankfully, they're heading the other way, so I grab Amira's arm and back up before they see us, my heart thumping harder with each step we take.

218

When we're safely around the corner, I turn to face her. "We'll go to another road. Find a way around them," I whisper.

She nods, her eyes growing even wider as the seconds tick by.

When I take off, jogging back the way we came and turning down a different road, she's right at my side. The sound of her heavy breathing is almost as loud as the scrape of the zombies' feet were a few minutes ago. It makes my heart rate soar to dangerous levels and has my eyes moving faster, searching every nook and cranny to make sure a horde of the undead doesn't jump us.

Two roads down, we turn so we are once again heading toward the wall. The way seems clear, even if the smell of death hangs heavy in the air, so I don't slow. Instead I pump my legs faster, keeping my eyes open and my focus on Amira's safety.

When a zombie stumbles out into the road in front of us, I raise the AK-47 and take aim as I move. There's just one, and even though a small voice inside me says to let it go or take it out with my knife, I don't want to disrupt the progress we're making. I squeeze the trigger, and the crack of the gunshot echoes through the quiet city, bouncing off the walls of the buildings around us. Probably making it tough for anything listening to be able to tell where the sound came from.

At least that's what I tell myself.

Amira grabs my arm, but I keep going, practically dragging her with me. When three more zombies stumble out of the alley in front of us, I'm ready to fire again. The wall is so close now that the risk seems worth it. All we have to do is make it to the end of the street and we'll be there.

I fire again, three shots in quick succession, and the zombies hit the ground. At my side Amira yelps, and I grab her hand, moving faster. Pumping my legs. Pulling her with me.

We reach the end of the street and the wall is right in front of us, so close I can touch it. I do, running my hand along the massive storage container that makes up this little section of the wall. Above it, more are stacked, and even more sit to the right and the left. Maybe fifty feet away, the makeup of the wall changes. There it's made of smashed cars and trucks, stretching out in front of us until they intersect with an old warehouse.

But there's no entrance into the city. No door that I can see.

"Fuck!" I scream, spinning around to look the other way, then back the way I was just looking. "How do we get in?"

Amira pulls on my arm, and I whirl around to find a massive horde of zombies barreling down on us. My heart jumps to my throat as I lift my rifle and aim, firing a few times and taking out who knows how many zombies before I grab Amira and run, heading toward the warehouse.

Our feet scrape against the pavement, and behind us zombies growl and moan. I keep running, but as far as I can see there's no way to get into the city, so I'm not sure where I'm going.

"Son of a bitch!" I yell, moving faster. Pulling Amira with me.

We reach the warehouse and are forced to go around it, squeezing down an alley that's jammed full of scrap metal and other long-ago rusted items. Amira trips and lets out a squeal, her knees slamming into the ground just before I jerk her back to her feet and force her to keep moving.

When we rush out onto the open road once again, we're faced with even more wall. On and on it stretches, taking my breath away with its massive size. Amira gasps next to me, and I look over my shoulder toward the horde. Trying to decide what to do. Behind us, they make their way through the alley, tripping over debris with almost every step, but not giving up. Their jaws snapping as they chomp at the air. Their hands reaching.

When I turn back to face the wall, I let out a deep breath, forcing my heart to calm down so I can focus. There has to be a way over. The smashed cars piled up in front of me are jagged and threatening, with glass and metal sticking out in so many areas it looks like the cars are just waiting to slice us to pieces. But with the zombies on one side and the never-ending expanse of the wall on the other, I'm not sure we have a choice. It's climb or keep running, and if we keep going, I'm afraid that sooner or later we'll hit a dead end.

I grab Amira and spin her around to face me. "We have to climb. Understand?"

She only nods once before I shove her toward the wall.

CHAPTER THIRTY

AMIRA

My feet stumble over each other when Jim gives me a push, but I throw my hands out, refusing to let myself fall. My palms slam into the hot surface of the smashed car in front of me, but I barely have time to register the heat before I'm pulling myself up. My hand gripping the hood of a car while I use a side view mirror as a foothold. Jim stays on the ground until I've climbed higher than his head, and then he too has boosted himself up. He climbs next to me, grinding his teeth together as the rifle sways behind him.

I gasp for breath and dig my hands in, ignoring the pain and the way my arms and legs tremble. Even though I'm dying to know what's going on, I only venture one quick look at the ground below us. The zombies have converged on the wall, their rancid teeth chomping as they reach for us.

Dying to get their claws into our skin. It's enough to make me move faster.

Even though my arms ache the whole way up, I reach the top in no time. I let out a cry of frustration as I haul myself up, landing on my stomach. Beneath me, the metal is so hot against my skin it feels like I'm being burned alive. I'm gasping and drenched in sweat, and my arms and legs are trembling.

Jim pulls himself up just as I get to my feet. Under me, the cars sway, and the hot Georgia wind slams into me so hard that it threatens to throw me over, but I'm able to see all the way across the city on both sides. The Atlanta we just braved stretches out before me, empty on most streets while others crawl with the dead. Swarms of them like swarms of insects out looking for the leftover crumbs from a picnic.

In the opposite direction, the world seems peaceful and clean. Fresh, even. Within the wall of new Atlanta, people stroll down the streets. Cars drive, and I even spot a couple children playing a game of basketball. It's like another world, and it's so shocking after all these months that I have the urge to close my eyes and rub them. Maybe even pinch myself. It just doesn't seem like something that could really exist. Not anymore.

Jim wraps his hand around my wrist, trying to get my attention, but I have a hard time ripping my eyes away from the sight in front of me. When I do, I find him smiling. Grinning like he's a kid again and he has his whole life in front of him.

"We made it."

I nod so hard my hair flies across my face, momentarily blinding me.

When I shove it aside, Jim's lips are moving again. *"...go this way. Maybe we'll find a lookout tower or something."*

He nods to the right before slipping his hand into mine, and then we're walking. Picking our way across the smashed cars that make up this wall in search of a way down.

Jim's right. It makes sense that they'd have some kind of tower, and it would probably be easier to look for it than to climb down to the other side. We made it up okay, but the jagged metal and broken glass could have been deadly.

We've only made it across three cars before Jim stops. He rubs his arm, and I suddenly feel like the most selfish person in the world. In the midst of the zombies and climbing the wall, as well as finding out that this new Atlanta is in fact a real thing, I had totally forgotten about Jim's injury. It must have really hurt when he climbed up.

"Are you okay?" My words vibrate through my head, and I can't help wondering if I'm yelling.

Jim doesn't flinch when he looks back at me, though. *'"Just sore."* He jerks his head to the right again. *"Let's keep moving."*

We pick our way along the wall, and it doesn't take long for what appears to be a tower to come into view. The sun is so bright that I have to shield my eyes. When I do, I see not just one, but two guard towers, and between them is what appears to be the entrance to the city. Just the sight of that door makes my heart fly into the air. Even though we are on top of this wall, there is a part of me that really hasn't accepted that we are safe. Not yet.

I want to run, but the way the wall shifts under my feet forces me to keep my pace steady. Jim looks back and grins, and I return his smile. My heart races in an excited rhythm that I haven't felt since before the virus killed most of the people on this planet.

There is hope after all.

Out of nowhere, Jim stops walking and lifts his hands. He glances over his shoulder, his eyes huge and his lips moving so fast I don't catch a single word. Then he steps in front of me, blocking my view and making my heart stutter. It only takes a second for it to hit me that I should have my hands up, too. When I lift them, I venture a look around Jim, only to find several guards heading our way, crossing the wall of smashed cars. Pointing guns at us as they scream words I can't make out. Their faces are so red and angry that it leaves no doubt in my mind about what's happening, though. We are in deep shit.

Jim is yanked forward, and his rifle is ripped away two seconds before a hand wraps around my arm. My own gun is pulled from my hand, and then I'm yanked forward. My feet trip across the wall, but the solider holding me never lessens his grip enough to allow me to fall. Jim's hands are still in the air, and as long as they're up, I keep mine raised. The guards wear helmets, making it tough for me to read their lips, but their body language screams at me with every move they make.

We reach the end of the wall, and a second later I find myself climbing down a ladder next to the guard tower. My hands tremble, and my palms are so sweaty that I'm terrified I'm going to lose my grip and go crashing to my death, but somehow I manage to make it to solid ground. Jim is there, his blue eyes big and round as he talks to the men but his lips are not facing me.

Is he intentionally trying to keep his words from me?

From out of nowhere, more guards show up, and everyone is talking at once. Their bodies jerk as their lips move, so fast and so many of them that I can't focus. Jim's hands are still raised as words I can't understand fly from his mouth. One of the men turns his gun on me and shouts something, but again I don't catch it, thanks to the damn helmet blocking most of his face.

Jim steps in front of me, and I can only assume he tells the men in front of us that I'm deaf, but it's impossible to know because all I can see is his back.

What seems like seconds later, Jim is jerked forward, and another man wraps his hand around my upper arm and pulls me toward a truck. It's the kind that used to make deliveries, like a UPS truck, but white instead of brown.

Jim and I are herded into the back like cattle, and my heart, which has already doubled its rhythm, pounds harder. The inside of the truck is dark and bare, the cold floor unforgiving against my knees. Jim crawls forward right in front of me, and I follow, stealing glances at the men who rounded us up but getting nowhere when I try to read their lips.

The men aren't paying attention to us anymore, and even though it's a relief, I can't relax yet. I don't have a clue what's going on, and I won't until I'm able to talk to Jim.

When we reach the back of the truck, he pulls me against him. I want to ask him what's happening, but I know it would be a waste of energy. The thick shadows surrounding us would make it impossible for me to read his lips.

Instead, I scoot closer and rest my head against his chest, placing my cheek right over his beating heart. The rhythmic thump is soothing in a way that nothing else can be right now. We're both alive, and I have to have faith that we'll stay that way. These men are just being cautious. That's all this is.

A couple men climb in with us, and a second later the door is pulled shut, covering us in a thick blanket of darkness. Then the truck lurches forward, bouncing over the uneven road, and Jim's arms tighten around me.

I try to tell myself that we're going to be okay, but I have no idea if it's true. Hopefully, saying it to myself enough will help keep me calm.

Less than five minutes after we start driving, the truck slows to a stop. I hold my breath, and under my ear, Jim's chest vibrates. He must be talking to the men. It's reassuring, knowing that they're at least communicating a little. Jim shifts and gets to his knees, slipping his hand into mine. He doesn't move, though, almost like he's waiting for something to happen. Maybe for the door to open?

That thought has barely entered my mind when all at once, light floods the back of the truck, blinding me. I squint, and a second later, Jim moves forward. He pulls me with him, giving my hand a reassuring squeeze as we move toward the open door.

My eyes haven't totally adjusted when we step out, but I can't miss the CDC. It looms in front of us, big and shiny, the windows reflecting the sun so brilliantly that I can't look directly at it. All around it, men and women walk in and out. Some armed, some not. Some wearing white coats while others talk in groups like it's just an ordinary day and there are no zombies. No death. No men herding people to the CDC like they are nothing more than animals.

Despite the guns and men surrounding Jim and me, seeing something that resembles normalcy helps calm me. We're in Atlanta. There is a wall. There are people working toward something permanent. Even if I don't understand their methods, that doesn't mean I'm in danger.

The soldiers move, once again corralling us forward. Jim never lets go of my hand, but the pace is rushed and hectic, and the guns so close to us that I don't have time to ask him what's happening. We move so fast that my feet practically trip over each other, and I feel like I have to run to keep up. Even then, someone will occasionally give me a little shove. Whether it's meant as a threat or encouragement to keep moving, I'm not sure.

When we walk into the lobby, the armed men finally stop. I look around, trying to take everything in at once, and find one of the men talking into a radio. His eyes meet mine. They're clear and blue and not the least bit threatening, and I relax. This is going to be okay. We are going to be okay.

For the first time since we got out of the truck, Jim's hand leaves mine. He grabs my shoulders and spins me around so I'm facing him. I blink, focusing on his mouth as it moves.

"We're here. Don't worry. This is just a precaution. They put everyone in quarantine when they first arrive."

Quarantine?

I open my mouth to ask how long they intend to keep us in quarantine, but before I can say anything, a hand wraps around my arm and Jim is ripped away from me. He's pulled in one direction, while a second man drags me another way. I scream what should be his name, but I'm not sure if that's how it comes out. Not that it matters. No one cares.

Jim struggles against the men pulling him forward, his mouth moving like crazy and his gaze locked on mine. They manage to get him turned around, and then he's being pulled through a door and dragged away. Gone.

My feet skid across the floor as the men pull me in another direction. I struggle, but it doesn't take much for them to overpower me. I'm too small to put up much resistance, and no matter what I do, they just keep moving until I, too, am dragged through a door.

I'm pulled down a sterile, white hallway, the fluorescent lights above us brighter than I'm used to after all these months of no electricity. My pupils dilate, trying to adjust to the artificial light, and I have to run to keep up with these men.

Through a window on my right, I catch sight of a lab. Rows and rows of tables with microscopes and other equipment that scream medical research. That must be where they're trying to create the vaccine. They're trying to do good. There's nothing for me to worry about.

My pounding heart says otherwise.

I'm pulled into a room that resembles a doctor's office, and the men finally release me. I spin around to face them, my eyes wild as I search for a way out, but there's nothing. The man on the right shakes his head and his lips move as he says something to the other man, but he isn't facing me, so I don't know what it is.

The second man nods, then turns my way. He gives me a smile that looks totally rehearsed and not at all friendly, and then he waves toward the table. When his lips move again, they're slower. *"It's okay. We're not here to hurt you. Take a seat. The doctor will be in soon."*

Doctor?

All I can picture is some mad scientist. White, unkempt hair and crazy eyes. He'll strap me down and perform experiments on me. Probably even inject me with the zombie virus so they can test out their drugs. That's what would happen in a movie, anyway.

I don't move, and the guard who told me to sit down frowns. *"Can you understand me? Your friend said you could read lips."*

Jim told them I was deaf, but he also told them I could read lips. Damn. I'd prefer to sit here silently and let them think I don't know what's going on. That way, they'll let their guard down. If they're hiding something, I want to know what it is before this *doctor* gets here.

I blink and stare at the guard for a second before moving my gaze to the other one.

He rolls his eyes. *"She doesn't know what the hell is going on. That asshole lied."*

I tilt my head and blink again.

"Whatever." The second guard waves to the table, making his movements so dramatic that I have the urge to kick him in the balls. *"Sit. Down."*

Even though I want to stay standing, I do what he says. With as exaggerated as his movements are, even a moron would be able to understand what he's saying.

The first guard rolls his eyes again, and the second one chuckles. They start talking, acting like I'm not even here. Which is fine with me.

I shift a little, trying to get a better view of their lips but trying to keep the movement subtle. I don't want them to know I'm taking it all in.

"Can't wait for this shift to be over," the first one says.

"No shit." The second one glances at me. *"At least we had a little excitement today. Usually it's just days and days of watching the cabbage guy."*

"You've been on cabbage duty?" The first guy shakes his head. *"They won't even let me near his room."*

"*Yeah. Although he's not a vegetable anymore. Up and walking around. Always looking for a fight. That asshole needs a guard.*"

They turn, still talking, making it impossible for me to read their lips. Not that it matters. I have serious doubts that I'm getting it all. Cabbage? Why the hell would they be talking about vegetables?

I cough, hoping they'll turn my way again, but the most I get is a glare from the first guy. He looks at me like he thinks I'm a waste of space.

A couple minutes pass before the door opens and a woman walks in. Her white coat says she's a doctor, but she's missing the crazy gleam in her eyes that I was expecting. If anything, she looks bored.

"*This is the girl?*" she asks the two guards.

Their heads bob, but they aren't facing me so I'm not sure what they're saying.

The doctor glances my way, her brown eyes sweeping over me. Slowly. Her blonde hair is pulled back into a ponytail, tight against her head, and the skin around her eyes is puffy. Like she hasn't gotten a lot of sleep lately. She doesn't look old, early forties at the most, but she carries herself like someone important. Like she knows the weight of the world rests on her shoulders.

I shift and glance away, uncomfortable under her penetrating gaze, but keep her in the corner of my eye.

When she looks back at the men, she says, "*Can she read lips?*"

The second guard looks over his shoulder, his lips already moving. "*–didn't get anything out of her. Not sure I'm doing it right. I –* " He turns away and I miss the rest of it.

The doctor steps past the men, nodding at me as she talks. "*You can wait in the hall.*"

The guards hurry out, obviously anxious to do something more interesting than guarding a dumb deaf girl.

When the doctor stops in front of me, she smiles. Even though it doesn't quite reach her eyes, I don't get the impression that she's dangerous or threatening. Just ready to move on.

"I'm Dr. Helton. Your friend told the other guards you were deaf but that you can read lips."

"I can." Even though I'm not ready to let my guard down completely, Jim already told them the truth about that one.

A smile spreads across the doctor's face as she takes a seat, moving her chair to face me. *"You were pretending with the guards?"*

"I wanted to know what I was in for."

"We aren't going to hurt you. I know this is probably more overwhelming for you than it is for others, but I promise this is standard procedure. We have to make sure we don't let anyone in who is infected."

"Why don't you tell me what you're going to do so I can make up my own mind?"

The doctor nods once. *"Fair enough. We draw some blood and do a physical exam to make sure there are no bites or scratches that could have infected you with the virus. If you're clean, you simply have to stay in quarantine for forty-eight hours."*

That sounds reasonable, but I'm not ready to let her off the hook yet. I want to know what they're doing here and why all the drama of dragging Jim away from me.

"And if I am infected?"

"Are you?" Her eyebrow cocks up.

"No, but I still want to know what standard procedure is."

"That seems reasonable." She sits back and crosses her arms, more relaxed now that I'm cooperating. *"If someone infected comes in, we wait to see if they turn. If they do, they're disposed of in the most humane way possible. We're hoping to find more people who are immune, but so far we've only found the one."*

Something flashes in her brown eyes that says she's lying, but about which part, I'm not sure. The humane part, or the part where they've only found one person who is immune?

"Jim knew someone who was immune. They were together, back in Colorado. Is he here now?"

That thing flashes in the doctor's eyes again. *"Jim knew Angus James?"*

Angus? What kind of a name is that?

"I don't know his name, I just know that he was with Jim."

Dr. Helton nods. *"Angus came in with a group of people a little over a month ago, but he was seriously injured when he arrived. We did what we could, but when we realized we couldn't save him, we put him in a coma so we could still use his blood to develop the vaccine. I realize it sounds cruel, but it was necessary. For the good of the human race."*

"He's dead, though? This Angus?" I hadn't expected that. When you hear that a person is immune, they almost seem superhuman.

The doctor nods again, her eyes holding mine. *"Yes. Very much so."*

I see that thing flash in her eyes again, but I'm still not sure where it came from or what it means. Maybe she isn't telling the truth. At least not the whole truth, anyway.

"That's too bad," I say.

"Yes, it is." Dr. Helton stands and motions for me to do the same. *"Let's get your exam over with so we can get you settled in. You'll have a room and a place to get cleaned up. After forty-eight hours, you can see Jim again."*

I stand and meet her gaze, trying to get a better read on her. She just blinks, and it's so slow I have to wonder if she isn't going to fall asleep standing up. Maybe it was just exhaustion or frustration I saw in her eyes before. Maybe she wasn't lying at all.

CHAPTER THIRTY-ONE

JIM

The shower did nothing to calm me, and neither did the clean clothes. The pants are stiff and scratchy against my skin as I move across the room. The only noise is the slap of my bare feet against the floor and the whoosh of the air conditioning as it blows cold air into the room. I should be thankful to have it blowing down on me after weeks of suffering through the sticky Georgia summer, but it just makes me feel trapped.

The throb from the gunshot wound hasn't lessened, but it's the ache inside me that is really unsettling. I rub my chest, but every time I think about Amira, the pain gets worse. They said this was normal and that we'd see each other in forty-eight hours, but the more time that passes, the more I start to wonder if I should have brought her here at all. Maybe she was right. Maybe her house was safer.

I sift through everything that happened since those guards spotted us on top of the wall. They raised their guns right away, and even though I tried to stay calm, it scared the shit out of me. They wouldn't stop yelling, and every time they tried to talk to Amira I would tell them she couldn't hear what they were saying, but they wouldn't stop. It took them way longer than it should have to figure out what I meant. Then they swept us into the truck with almost no information about what to expect, and warning bells started going off in my head like crazy.

Still, I tried to stay calm, but the last straw was them separating Amira and me. My fist still aches from the black eye I gave the bastard who dragged me through that door, and my side won't stop throbbing from the blow he gave back. They just kept telling me to stay calm even though they wouldn't tell me a damn thing about where they took Amira. As if that was even possible.

My back is to the door when it clicks open, and I spin around so fast that I nearly lose my balance.

The woman standing in the doorway freezes and lifts her hands like she's trying to hold me back, and when I don't move, she nods toward the bed at my side. "I'd feel better if you took a seat."

"I'm not here to make you feel better."

"I didn't say you were, but the guards thought I'd need an escort. I assured them that you were a reasonable person and that wouldn't be necessary. You only reacted the way you did because you weren't sure what was going on." She lifts one eyebrow, her head still tilted toward the bed. "Am I right?"

"You're half right," I say. "Violence isn't a new thing for me, but I wouldn't have punched that asshole if he hadn't dragged Amira away."

"That's what I thought." Her eyes flit toward the bed, but she doesn't move as she waits for me to decide what I'm going to do.

Sitting isn't going to put me in any more danger than I'm already in, and it sure as hell would be a lot more comfortable than pacing this damn room. Still, I hesitate for a few seconds just to make the woman in front of me squirm.

It works. She shifts from foot to foot and clears her throat. When her gaze moves to the door, I take it as my cue to sit, but I take my time strolling across the room. Letting her know I'm doing it for my own benefit. Not hers.

The bed creaks under me when I lower myself onto it, nearly drowning out the sigh of relief the doctor lets outs. "Thank you."

"Don't thank me yet. I'm only cooperating so you can give me some answers."

The doctor nods once before crossing the room and taking a seat in a chair opposite me. "You were already told that you'd be in quarantine for forty-eight hours. It's standard procedure to split men and women up until we can make sure things are…okay." Her mouth tightens. "We've had groups come in that weren't as friendly as they let on."

Even though her explanation makes sense—and rings true with some of the shit Jon told me back in Hope Springs—there's nothing comforting about it. I won't be able to really relax until Amira is standing in front of me and I'm able to make sure she's all right.

"So Amira is okay?"

"She is. I just did her exam. No major injuries or bites. We do a standard round of blood work on everyone who comes in, but we won't have the results for that right away. She—"

"Why blood work? What are you looking for?"

"You of all people should know." The doctor doesn't even blink. "Amira said you were acquainted with Angus James."

"So they made it?" I've been dying to know, but with everything else going on, I haven't had the chance to ask. "Angus, Axl, and Vivian. What about the baby?"

"The group came in a few weeks ago. The brothers, Vivian, Parvarti, Joshua, and the baby. Megan. You were with them?"

I sit back a little, the relief nearly taking my breath away with its intensity. All these weeks of wondering if my sacrifice helped them. A part of me thought I'd never find out for sure.

"Left Colorado with them," I say after a moment. "We lost a lot along the way."

"So I heard." She sighs and shakes her head, and my whole body stiffens. "I wish I had better news to give, but I don't. Angus is dead. He made it here just before he died, so his blood will help create a vaccine. At least that's the hope."

"Shit." I shake my head. "Axl must have taken it hard. They were as close as two brothers can be."

"He was able to say goodbye, at least." I look up when the doctor stands, but she doesn't meet my gaze head on. "I have a lot to do, but I'll be sure to let your friends know you've arrived. Until then, we have the preliminary exam to do, as well as the blood work. I'd also like to take a look at your arm. I hear you were shot?"

"Yeah." I rub the muscle under the gunshot almost absentmindedly.

"If you don't mind, I'd like to get it done."

"Sure." I get to my feet, my mind still spinning from all the new information. "Let's get it over with."

FORTY-EIGHT HOURS DRAGS WHEN YOU'RE ALONE, making me appreciate what Amira faced those five days she was by herself even more. Still, it gives me a chance to rest up and allows my arm to heal a little. It's still tender, but by the time the guards come to let me out of my cell, I can move my arm without wincing.

They lead me down the same halls I was brought in, past closed doors and dark labs before finally stopping in front of a door very similar to the one I just came out of. I shift, shooting them looks that they ignore while they type a code into the keypad.

When the door finally clicks open, I nearly push them out of the way as I rush inside. The room is just like mine. The only difference is the girl lying on the bed. Her eyes are closed, but I can tell by the way her fingers pick at the blanket that she isn't asleep. She just didn't hear the door open.

Like me, she's clean and wearing new clothes. Her dark hair is spread out across the bed, fanning her face. When I lower myself onto the bed at her side, her body stiffens. She cracks one eye, and a split second later she's in my arms, throwing her little body against mine so hard that a throb moves up and down my arm.

"Jim!" Her voice booms through the small room, loud enough to make my eardrums vibrate, but I don't care because I couldn't be happier to see a person than I am right now.

I pull back so I can look her in the eye, taking all of her in. "How are you?"

"Bored out of my damn mind. You?" Her gaze moves to my arm. "Are you healing?"

"Had lots of time to heal and sleep, and now all I want to do is be with you." I wink. "Preferably naked."

A flush spreads across her cheeks, and her eyes move to the door where the two guards stand waiting. Just seeing them reminds me of all the things we have waiting for us. Finally, after all these weeks, I can see Axl and the others. Find out what happened to them after I ran out of that farmhouse and reassure myself that Megan is okay. Plus, I was told that Amira and I would have an apartment. Just thinking about that has me remembering the promise I made.

"Come on." I stand, taking her with me as I head for the door, walking sideways so she can read my lips. "I promised you that when we got here, we'd spend the next two days in bed, but this wasn't what I had in mind."

The expression on her face tells me she only caught half of what I said, but I don't stop.

"You ready?" the guard at the door asks, sounding bored out of his mind.

"Get me out of this damn building."

I hold Amira's hand as we follow the guards, winding our way through a labyrinth of identical hallways until we finally make it out into the lobby. It's early afternoon and the building is crowded with people, some wearing white coats while others are dressed as guards.

The two men in charge of our transport stop only two steps into the lobby, and one of them waves across the room. "Over there. You have people waiting for you."

"Thanks," I mutter as I slip my arm around Amira's shoulder.

I don't have to ask who it is. The doctor told me my friends would be waiting, and there they are. Axl, Vivian, Parvarti, Joshua, and Megan. On top of that, Lila and Al are standing there, smiling like crazy. The last time I saw them was before we jumped into that river, and I sure as hell didn't expect to find them standing here now.

"You made it!" Vivian steps forward, cradling Megan in her arms.

The baby is so much bigger. Logically, I knew it would happen, but seeing her reminds me of how much time has actually passed. They must have thought I'd never make it here. Hell, there were times when I started to doubt that we'd find our way.

"It was touch and go—" I slip my arm around Amira's shoulders. "—but I'm a fighter."

Vivian's smile is bittersweet when she says, "We almost gave up hope."

"Made a detour. This is Amira. I'd be dead if she hadn't found me." I nod toward the girl at my side who saved me more than once.

Amira smiles as I introduce her to everyone, feeling a little bit like I'm dreaming. It doesn't seem real, being here in front of these people and knowing there are no zombies walking the streets right now. No one is going to rush in and try to kill us. We aren't going to starve, and we don't have to try to figure out where our next meal is coming from. Thanks to the sacrifice Angus James made, the CDC is working on a vaccine, meaning babies like Megan will have a future ahead of them. It's almost crazy.

"I can't imagine what you went through," Lila says, leaning against Al. "The world out there is terrifying."

Amira shudders, and I know she's thinking about her dad. I tighten my arm around her and give her a little squeeze.

"You don't have to tell us."

My eyes meet Axl's, who until now has been silent.

"I heard Angus didn't make it."

Axl nods slowly, and his eyes move to the ground when his mouth scrunches up. "Got the chance to say goodbye, that's somethin'." He shakes his head. "He was in a coma, but they say people can hear you when they're like that. Hope so."

Amira perks up at my side, but when her gaze meets mine, I shake my head and mouth, *I'll tell you all about it later.*

It's been weeks and weeks, but I'm sure the wound is still raw, and I don't want to drag Axl through that again. Especially not when this should be a happy reunion.

"They say we'll have an apartment?" I ask.

"Right down the hall from us." Vivian adjusts the baby on her hip. "We can show you."

"So this place is really as good as they claim?" Amira asks, speaking for the first time. Her brown eyes are shining, and I swear to God I've never seen her look so damn beautiful.

"It's not perfect," Vivian says. "Then again, nothing ever was. The important thing is that they're trying. Not just here, but in other areas. One day we might have something real again."

Something real. For the first time in my whole life, I feel hope swell in my chest. I've never looked at the future and thought I could have any kind of life worth living, but now, standing in Atlanta with Amira at my side, I do. I can see it, though. Amira and me, a family. Nothing will ever be perfect, but compared to anything I've ever had before, this will be the closest I'll ever come.

I slide my hand down Amira's arm and turn her my way. "You and I, we have something real right here. Right now."

She smiles back up at me, her eyes lighting up like she can see it too. Damn, I can't wait to be alone with her. To take my time and know nothing is going to swoop in and destroy our moment together.

I turn back to face my friends. "I'd love to see that apartment now, if you don't mind."

The others nod. They turn and head for the door, and I follow. My arm around Amira, pulling her with me. Every step we take, I feel more confident in our future here. Together.

Acknowledgements

A special thanks goes out to my brother, Clint, for helping me out with my gun questions when I had them. It was never really important to me that I didn't have specifics about the weapons the survivors were using, but after my brother took the time to read my books, something I never though he'd do since he isn't much of a reader, I thought I should humor him by adding those details. The M1 carbine Amira uses has special meaning because it was our grandpa's favorite gun, something I wouldn't have known if my brother hadn't told me.

Thanks also to Jen Naumann and Erin Rose for being my first readers. A huge thank you goes to Laura Johnsen, Carey Monroe, and Mary Jones for searching the manuscript for typos and Emily Teng for once again editing for me.

To all the fans who patiently waited for another book, but never gave up hope, thank you. I'm glad you all enjoyed this series enough to beg for more, and I'm happy that Jim's story came out so easily. I had fun writing it and, as usual, I enjoyed having the opportunity to write from the perspective of someone totally new and different from myself.

About the Author

Kate L. Mary is an award-winning author of New Adult and Young Adult fiction, ranging from Post-apocalyptic tales of the undead, to Speculative Fiction and Contemporary Romance. Her Young Adult book, *When We Were Human*, was a 2015 Children's Moonbeam Book Awards Silver Medal winner for Young Adult Fantasy/Sci-Fi Fiction, and a 2016 Readers' Favorite Gold Medal winner for Young Adult Science Fiction. Don't miss out on the *Broken World* series, an Amazon bestseller and fan favorite.

For more information about Kate, check out her website: www.KateLMary.com

CPSIA information can be obtained
at www.ICGtesting.com
Printed in the USA
FSHW011253071218
54317FS